ORIGINAL SIN

AGOSTINO CRIME FAMILY: A PREQUEL

DAHLIA REIGN

Dear readers,

As usual, I must forewarn that triggers—do in fact—lie within these pages. Xoxo, D.

ABOUT THE BOOK

My last name might have been Agostino. But to the people of New York, I was the death of mafia tradition and the face of change.

The city was Mario Agostino's by birthright. But that didn't mean his reign would be met without opposition. Blood coated the streets, alliances were tested, new enemies crawled out of the shadows. Everyone wanted a cut. A taste of something that didn't belong to them.

Even if that something came in the form of a woman. An arranged marriage. A wife who was no better than a stranger.

It didn't take Mario long to realize Isabella Bruno was so much more than that. The union offered him money, power, reach beyond his wildest dreams. Making the man untouchable. If only he could trust his new bride… If only he could trust… *anyone*.

Every story had to start somewhere. The Agostinos just happened to come wrapped in sin.

Welcome to the origins of New York City's most powerful mafia family.

PROLOGUE
MARIO-PRESENT

My hands firmly gripped her neck, the delicate muscles pulling taut beneath my hold. And I watched on as exhaustion was slowly replaced by terror. A man of my power—caliber—didn't tolerate a woman's disobedience. Their punishment was often simple, but in this case, she deserved the worst.

She'd tried to throw me to the wolves. The mutts constantly sniffing around, wanting to snuff out my reign. Being the head of *il famiglia* guaranteed me enemies. But it shouldn't be those closest to me putting the blade in my back.

"I don't believe your fuckin' lies." I snarled in her face, her eyes begging me to let her go. "You little bitch! How could you do this to me?" I flexed my hand and dumped her body at my feet as she heaved in labored breaths.

"Y-you don't kill women, Mario. I know you!" She curled up on her side, her makeup smeared and her sobs pathetic.

Gripping her hair, I tugged her head back, forcing her to look me in the face. "You *did* fucking know me. Which meant you should've kept your fuckin' mouth shut." I released my grip for a second time—the mere thought of her touch made me sick. "I want to know every-fucking-thing you told him."

"N-nothing. I swear, Mario!" Her lies flowed so easily I wanted to snap her neck.

I picked up a chair and threw it across the room.

"All right, calm down." Rick stood to the side—my best friend sounded amused where I was heated. "Either do it or don't, but let's go."

Why was it that those closest to me had the sharpest knives? All the women in my life had let me down. *She* was no different. The moment I looked away, she tried running to another city. To another boss.

But my reach far surpassed New York, and Philly was a friend. Thankfully.

"I just wanted your attention, Mario. That's all." She started kissing my shoes. "You're my everything. W-when you sent me away, I just wanted your attention."

"Well, you fuckin' got it, didn't you?"

"I'm sorry! She doesn't make you happy and that's why you spent all your time with me! I acted out and I wanted to apologize! But you wouldn't let me."

"Those drugs must be eating away at your brain. Acting like you're *someone* to me."

She wept harder when my hands combed through her hair, gripping tight before I dragged her into the back room as she fought against me.

"You fucked up."

"Please, I need to tell you… just let me explain!"

I deposited her crying, lying ass into the center of the locked room and smiled when she glanced at the drain dug into the cement floor. Then I lifted my hand, realization settling over her face as she stared down the barrel of my gun.

"Harder. Harder, please. Mario, I-I…" Serafina's tight pussy gripped me perfectly. "Yes!" And her nails ran down my back as she came on my dick.

"We ain't done yet." I pounded into her harder, needing to show her who owned her.

What a joke.

I didn't own shit. Not since my father arranged my marriage to another woman to create a powerful alliance with her old man. Serafina was my everything. And I'd tell her as much as soon as I finished fucking her.

The moment I stopped thrusting and came, she held my face in her hands. "What's wrong?"

"What'd you mean?"

"You seem a million miles away."

I rolled my hips, showing her I was still very much inside her.

"You know what I mean." She gave me one of her soft smiles.

Serafina had grown up in the mafia, our fathers stepping up around the same time. But where mine was doing well for himself, hers wasn't high up enough to broker an engagement with the future *capo*. Marriage was a tool used to garner more money—more power. And her family didn't have either.

"Had a meeting with my father…" I pulled my cock free and sat on the edge of the bed.

"Okay."

Serafina understood what my life was about, that there were things I didn't have control over. Like picking my future wife. The *famiglia* was rooted in tradition. Something we were hiding from. Ready to run to avoid.

"He's creating a new alliance." *Fuck, I hated this.* "There's this Sicilian family… Wealthy and they—"

She started to tear up before I could finish.

"Shit, come here."

Serafina slowly walked around the bed and into my embrace, resting her head on my chest. I squeezed her tight, knowing this confession would break us.

"How long?"

"Not long," I told her and dropped my hands when she pulled away from me.

She didn't want to admit it, but we both knew this was the alliance I needed. There were plenty of names out there, ready to take me out the moment my father stepped down. He was made for this life, true to his core, old mafia. I was the face of change and change was never good. Many would opt to keep things the way they were.

But this marriage? It came with money and with money came protection.

Serafina nodded while a sad smile played on her lips. "We always knew it would end this way. But a ring won't matter…"

"You're not some whore. You deserve to be happy, married, have a family of your own."

"I want that with *you*, Mario." The tears were silently streaming down her cheeks now. But I knew better. I saw past the grief, straight through to the rage.

Serafina Greco was hot-headed and didn't fall in line with the image of the traditional Italian daughter. My father would constantly comment that her family had no control over the girl. She was raised with a silver spoon and *without* obedience. There were never any repercussions for her actions. A woman was to be demure, to listen and do as she was told.

That wasn't Fina. Not in the slightest.

My face hardened. I needed to put her in her place. For her sake as much as mine. "I know. But it's done."

She fell into my arms. Serafina was a mess of emotions. She had a fierce temper and uncontrollable sadness. A dangerous combination. Especially when she wasn't getting what she wanted.

It made the make-up sex wild.

But that was all over now. My father was getting older, tired. It was time for him to retire. The plans I had in mind for *il famiglia* would take us to the next level. Make us untouchable. And this impending alliance was part of that plan.

"Is she pretty?" Serafina's tiny whisper chipped at a piece of my heart.

Why the fuck does she do this to herself?

"Stop, Fina." Nothing I said would soothe her, so there was no point in having this discussion. "I'll find someone who will protect you. Who will love you. Better than I can."

If I would have known that this would be one of the biggest lies I ever told, I would've shut my own fuckin' mouth. And I would've said nothing as I held her a little bit longer.

"I wish your mother was here to see this." My father wasn't an emotional man. Ever.

My Sicilian bride had arrived to the States late. Her father came to our meeting prior to the wedding, but she was kept away. He claimed that it was to protect her virtue. To protect her from me and the rumors he'd heard about me. Which was comical at best. Like I'd break the contract now or something.

I'd already said goodbye to the woman I could've seen myself marrying. So why the fuck would I tarnish my new bride before I put that ring on her finger?

My pops had ordered me to keep my mouth shut. While I was left to wonder how we were supposed to make an alliance with a man who didn't trust us. Who was handing over his daughter but didn't *trust us* until we'd signed on the dotted line?

The room was filled with around two hundred people. A mix of business associates and direct members of *the family*. All champing at the bit in hopes of seeing me break. Thinking I'd finally show some emotion.

I wouldn't give them shit. My name was feared for a reason.

The entrance song started, and I remained stoic as I waited for my wife to appear. A woman I'd yet to even meet. As my eyes bounced around the crowd of spectators, all here to witness this sham of a wedding, anger took hold. I wanted to reach behind my back, draw my weapon, and take aim. I wanted to fire and see where my bullets landed.

Serafina's father was positioned at the back of the room, having forbade his daughter from attending. He knew as well as I did that the girl was volatile. But we both also knew she wouldn't listen. I could feel her here somewhere. Watching. Meanwhile, my old man was in the front row with our entire line of made men. The other side barely spoke English. *Her family.*

As the doors opened, my palms itched to pull my gun. My father told me she was beautiful. Then again, I felt like he had to say that, seeing as I was holding on by a quickly unraveling thread.

Truth was, it didn't matter what the woman looked like. She'd never be Serafina. Pussy was pussy. I'd fuck her until she produced me an heir. And if it was tight, I'd consider fucking her afterwards as well.

But I had to admit I was a bit shocked as I watched the thin frame walking towards me with her old man on her arm. Her dress was simple and figure-hugging. I'd expected something over the top from someone of her standing. Her long veil was thick, and with each step she took in my direction, I felt my heart beating faster.

As they approached the end of the aisle, her father extended a hand. I shook it, squeezing hard enough to show the fucker I wasn't playing games. He met my glare with one of his own before whispering in his native tongue. "I get a single call. A letter. Anything telling me that you aren't treating her right… I'll crush this entire-fucking-city." Then he kissed the girl on the top of her head before handing her over to me.

I turned to face my mystery bride, still barely able to make out her features while the thick lace taunted me to rip it off. Minutes felt like an eternity as we pivoted towards the priest before he began the grueling affair of conducting a lengthy Roman Catholic wedding.

I didn't ask for this. None of it.

I was a little girl who once had so many dreams. Not of a prince and a happily ever after. But to see the world, to make a difference. I wanted to help those less fortunate. I wanted to go places not many had traveled.

I'd been born into a life of corruption. Forced into a marriage with a stranger. My father loved me. He promised me it would be a good match, that my husband would be a good man.

As if there were any good men in *il famiglia*.

I'd wanted love. Someone to commit to me because of *me*. Not because of what my father offered them in return. I'd had a duty as his daughter, but was it so much to ask for more?

Staring at my betrothed through my lace veil, I smiled to myself. He was handsome enough. Mario Agostino had a powerful jaw, good bone structure, thick dark hair, and intense steel-blue eyes.

Rich. Powerful. Handsome. He checked all the boxes.

And here I was, his blushing bride.

It didn't take a genius to realize the man in front of me was probably just as unhappy as I was. If the soft whimpers on his side of the pews were anything to go by, my competition was in this church. Attending my wedding. Crying for the man I was taking from them.

I'd heard whispers of the Agostino heir. His father might have started the empire, but the man beside me had taken it to new heights. Cutthroat. Dangerous. Manipulative. Those were just a few of the words used to describe my future husband. And my father happily handed me over to him.

I'd heard what Papa said and I knew he meant it. But I'd never call him. This was my one job. To marry into an alliance and produce the next generation of heirs. I smiled at that. I'd always wanted a large family. I'd been raised to be a strong, proper wife for a *made man*. My father knew I could handle myself, even if he'd kept me sheltered. Not just my virtue—but my entire existence. His enemies in Sicily had gotten their hands on me once, and he vowed he'd never allow someone to hurt me again. However, that sparked my need to never be lonely.

If my husband wanted to cheat, I'd survive. I just wanted a family, children who would love me unconditionally. That was all I needed to survive this. And maybe—hopefully—I'd be permitted to attend various charities and events. To help people in the way I always dreamed of doing. Even on some small level.

"*Viva gli sposi!*" The wedding guests shouted, stirring me out of my trance.

"*Puoi baciare la sposa!*" The priest smiled as Mario turned to me, gripping the veil.

Would he like what he saw? Would he be disgusted?

The moment the thick lace rose, my heart stalled. It was the first time those entrancing eyes focused on me. As if he could see through to my past, my present, and my future—reading into my most private thoughts. They dissected me and made me squirm.

His strong jaw tensed, and I loved the way a myriad of things settled between us. Warm, strong hands wrapped around my waist and pulled me to his muscular chest. Then he pressed a calloused finger to my chin, tilting my mouth towards him.

The kiss was warm and soft. The slightest gasp left me as his tongue traced the line of my lips. Just as quickly as it had started, it was over. Mario turned us to the crowd and well wishes erupted as he practically dragged me back down the aisle. We passed friends and family. So many smiles and so much excitement filled the room, my husband returning each gesture with a tight smile of his own.

But nothing more.

The butterflies in my stomach shouldn't be fluttering at the thought of him accepting me. Till death do us part was something our families took seriously. He'd accepted the arrangement and we were tied for life.

Mario glanced down at me, a strange look on his face, before he gave me a wink. My face warmed at his perusal. We'd slowed our descent towards the open doors as people rushed to greet us. Mario held onto my hand, thanking everyone as I smiled and spoke politely. There were so many faces and introductions. Everything blurred while my new husband stood at the open door, his rough hand in mine and his strong presence at my side. And I allowed myself a moment of contentment.

Maybe this could work...

Then the world slowed on its axis. The joyous sounds around me seemed to die off, and I felt the strangest sensation. Like someone was shooting daggers at me.

Have you ever felt a metaphorical blade slicing through your back? The sensation so visceral and agonizing after just one look?

My husband stood taller, his grip on my hand so tight it threatened to break bone. The strangest realization hit me as he turned and sort of... tucked me behind him.

I glanced around, searching out any possible threat. Papa was at ease, laughing with Mario's father. So why was my husband suddenly so alert?

Someone else leaned forward and pulled me in for a hug, drawing my attention. I smiled at the kind woman before turning back to Mario. I couldn't make out what was being said over the chatter of the crowd, but the exchange was terse. Papa and Mario's father corralled us to the waiting limos while beckoning everyone to the venue. Mario tugged me behind him and then I heard it. His words clear as day.

"Don't do this, Fina."

And then I was stumbling along with him, trying to catch myself. Until I felt that same piercing sensation crawling up my spine and quickly glanced behind me.

The woman was shorter in stature, but lithe with a nice figure. Her long chestnut hair was soft and billowy. And even with a look of disgust twisting up her features, there was no denying she was beautiful. Light skin and intense hazel eyes watching my every move.

Mario practically threw me into the waiting limo before storming around to the other door. Then he folded himself alongside me as I stared out the window.

Married for ten minutes and already my future was pitted in despair and loneliness. Because I knew it, without my new husband ever having to confirm it.

There she was.

The other woman in my marriage.

The woman who held my husband's heart.

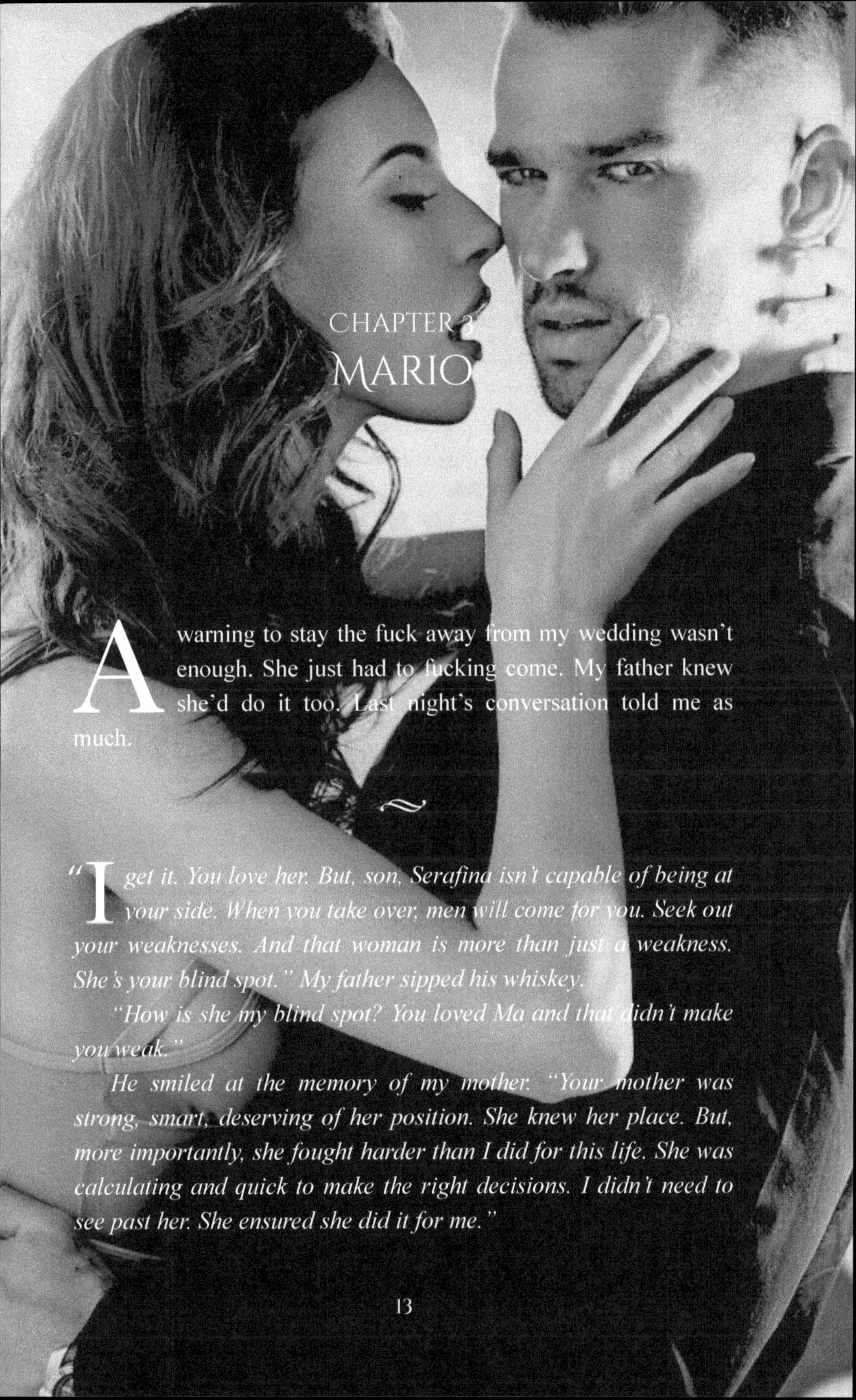

CHAPTER 3

MARIO

A warning to stay the fuck away from my wedding wasn't enough. She just had to fucking come. My father knew she'd do it too. Last night's conversation told me as much.

~

"I get it. You love her. But, son, Serafina isn't capable of being at your side. When you take over, men will come for you. Seek out your weaknesses. And that woman is more than just a weakness. She's your blind spot." My father sipped his whiskey.

"How is she my blind spot? You loved Ma and that didn't make you weak."

He smiled at the memory of my mother. "Your mother was strong, smart, deserving of her position. She knew her place. But, more importantly, she fought harder than I did for this life. She was calculating and quick to make the right decisions. I didn't need to see past her. She ensured she did it for me."

"And Fina won't be that for me?" Even as I asked the question, I knew the answer.

"You understand."

I hated that he was right. The direction I'd planned to take the family meant I needed someone capable of seeing the bigger picture. A woman who would not only give me heirs but alleviate my stress when I got home, not add to the pile of shit on my shoulders. A woman who knew her place and would follow my commands. Fina was none of those things. And as my father and I fell into comfortable silence, sipping whiskey and reading the file on my future wife, I knew what I had to do and why.

As much as I cared for her, Fina would only hinder my plans. Her rage would create more enemies, more problems for me to clean up. She was out of control and not even I could stop her when she was on a tear.

Maybe my betrothed would be a perfect match after all.

~

The sound of Fina's voice broke me from my thoughts. "She's beautiful." She was looking past me, her glare honed in on my new bride.

"I told you not to come," I hissed. "What the fuck were you thinking?"

"I wish you many years of happiness." The hollowness of her tone was disconcerting. There was nothing more terrifying than a woman with nothing left to lose. She was going to do something stupid. I knew it without having to know what that something was.

"Don't." It was both a plea and a warning as I watched her turn and walk away without acknowledgement.

My mood was wild, all over the place, as I tried to breathe through the rage while dragging my new wife to the car. Isabella was soft and demure as she folded her hands over her lap. I didn't know what I expected when she came down the aisle, but it wasn't… this. *Her.* Someone so understatedly beautiful.

When I'd pulled back that veil, I'd been ready for just about anything. A big-ass nose. Pocked skin. Bad teeth maybe. Not shiny, chestnut waves flowing down her back. Not kind eyes, which were like pools of dark honey and a smile equally sweet and timid. Isabella stood firm, her spine straightened by the authority she knew she possessed but there was an innate kindness beneath it all. And I was certain my men would see it too.

I slid inside the limo, leaning my back against the plush leather, my bride at my side and her attention out the window. Serafina was in the center of the crowd, staring at us as we pulled away. Blank. Withdrawn. Dangerous.

"She's… no one," I said after a few moments of tense silence.

Isabella didn't respond. Not until we were stopped outside my father's restaurant. Guests were already pouring inside, laughter filling the streets, while neither of us moved to follow them. "My only ask," she said as she slowly turned towards me, "is that you never lie to me. If I ask a question, if you tell me something, ugly or not, I expect it to be the truth."

"And if you don't like the answer?" I lifted a curious brow.

"Then I never should've asked the question in the first place and that's on me. You'll see I can handle this life. I was raised to do it. What I will not tolerate are lies in my home, under my roof."

That wasn't an unreasonable request. And I respected her forthrightness. I needed a partner in this life as much as I needed a woman to bend to my will. It was the foundation for what I was trying to build. Which was more of a punch to the gut than I wanted to admit at the time.

Truth was I'd wanted to fight this. Wanted to deny this marriage could be a good thing for the family. For me. Isabella seemed sensible where Serafina had a temper. A mean streak that meant she often disregarded the consequences of her actions. A powerful man and an unhinged woman meant disaster. Left me open to lose… everything.

"She's… someone," I attempted to clarify. Isabella understood my meaning without me having to say more.

"I'm under no illusion this will be a marriage founded by love and fidelity." Her words seared through me at the thought of someone else touching what was legally mine. "But thank you for the truth."

Isabella reached for the handle. I grabbed her arm to stop her. Even now she was the epitome of grace as she shrugged me loose and stepped out of the limo.

We entered together before Isabella headed towards the guests waiting to greet her. And I made a beeline for the bar. "About time, son." My father slapped me on the back. "Get a little taste in the limo?" He laughed and I forced out a low chuckle.

My newly appointed father-in-law was leaning against the bar. Watching me. The man was perceptive and my usual calm mask was close to slipping. Isabella had rattled me. She grew up in this life; she knew the score. But beneath her trained submission, I sensed her strength. Was intrigued by it more than I liked to admit.

Rick moved in next to me, handing me a whiskey as we stared at the crowd. My wife was being passed around the room while my family welcomed her with open arms. A bunch of sharks out for fucking blood. Even so, she held her own with a quiet elegance. Her every movement caught my attention. A simple flick of her wrist. Tilt of her neck. The challenge in her eyes. Isabella Agostino was a goddamn force to be reckoned with. And I wasn't sure my city was ready for her.

"I wonder if she's still as soft as she looks when she bleeds," Rick muttered under his breath, but it was loud enough to carry to her father's ears.

Michele Bruno was an enigma, much like my own father. The two men were known for their wraths. Even so, you didn't normally see *made men* so focused on their daughters. His stare was set to kill as he watched my best friend outwardly disrespect Isabella.

I glanced back at my wife, and she smiled when she caught me looking at her. Rubbing a hand over my heart, I smirked as I pushed against the beating organ.

Michele stepped closer without me realizing it. "She's something special. A good girl." He paused as if considering his next words. "It's you who needs this alliance, not me. My daughter and my money are all I've got. Which means I'll use every fucking penny I have to destroy your father, this city, and *you* if you fucking hurt her."

"Watch yourself, Michele." I understood his concern but the man needed to realize *she* belonged to me now. "She will be revered when I take over. She will be their *capo's* wife. But first and foremost, she is *mine*. This is about to be *my city*, so watch how you fucking speak to me."

"Gentlemen." Isabella stepped to my side, drawing our attention away from the harsh words shared between us and towards her. "May I steal my husband so dinner can be served?"

"My *bellissima figlia!* Yes, yes. Please. Let's eat." Michele kissed the top of his daughter's head before walking off with one final glare tossed over his shoulder. At me...

"I'm all he has left of my mother." Isabella watched her father walk off. "I will ensure he stays in line. Shall we?"

Who was this woman? And why was I so infatuated by her?

Isabella tugged at my arm, escorting me to our sweetheart table in the center of the room. I lowered myself onto the chair, leaned back, and watched our family and friends mill about. The staff moved quickly throughout the crowd while my wife sat quietly with her hands in her lap again. I'd pay anything to know what was going through her head. The way she'd handled Fina left me curious. Was it all a farce? Or was this woman, with the lingering fire in her eyes, really all she seemed to be.

Calm. Patient. *Tolerable.*

"She needs some wine," I instructed the waiter as he refilled my whiskey.

"No, thank you." Isabella's hands shook as she sipped her water.

"Wine, now." I waved the man off before turning to my wife. "You're nervous. It'll help."

"Or it'll make me sloppy." She dabbed at her mouth with a napkin before whispering, "Regretful."

Before I could ask her what she meant, the waiter had returned. Isabella stared at the glass like it might bite her while I tossed my drink back and ordered another. I hated how I couldn't stop looking at her. She smiled when it was appropriate, shook hands, and engaged flawlessly. The guests read my face and moved past me quickly. And I continued to watch her until I got my fill.

It was the way the muscles in her delicate neck moved whenever she swallowed. The slight twitch of her eye when she smiled. And worse, the way she wrung her hands in her lap whenever she was nervous. The Italian princess appeared unbothered to the untrained eye.

But I knew better.

Isabella cut her meat precisely, wiped her hand on the napkin in her lap, and took the tiniest bites. Her restraint was remarkable but I wanted to see her unravel. I wanted to know what it looked like when she let loose. I wanted to see her face when I ripped pleasure from her. How her muscles worked when she choked on my cock.

I made no promises to behave. It wasn't in my nature. And given the chance, I *could* easily break her neck. Just like I planned to break that thin strand of membrane between her thighs. Needing. Wanting her to bleed for me. She was my wife in name, but I'd craved to see her on her knees. Submitting to me in the bedroom as well.

Reaching under the table, I gripped her shaking hands in my own. Her skin was soft and delicate.

"Congratulations, my friend." The new boss of Philly stepped forward. And my grip instantly tightened on Isabella without me meaning to do it.

Metro and I had settled into a tentative peace since we were both getting married and taking over our cities at the same time. I pushed to my feet and reached across the table to accept his extended palm. My eyes drifted to the woman at his side. His new wife. Dressed in a designer gown far too tight and revealing with a painted-on face. She seemed to walk with her nose permanently in the air. And, once again, I found myself thankful for the girl seated beside me.

Our wives couldn't be more different. It seems my father did me a favor when he chose my bride.

Isabella came around, ignoring the other woman's scowl, and introduced herself to Metro. He complimented her beauty, kissing her cheeks as he whispered Italian sentiments. Where my wife was polite and reserved, his openly perused my body.

"*Abbastanza!*" Metro grunted in her direction.

"It was nice meeting you. Perhaps one day we can come visit your city," Isabella interjected, the lull of her voice effectively calming him. "I hear the history is incredible. *Grazie per essere venuto.*"

"It would be my pleasure. And congratulations again." Metro pivoted on his heel, a natural smile flicked in Isabella's direction as he yanked his wife behind him.

"Let's dance." I guided Isabella away from the table before she could protest.

"Everything came together beautifully," she hummed while her tight-set jaw told me otherwise. "Do you like it?" She was looking at everything but me.

"Beautiful." My tone was dark and deep.

"Wish I could've planned some of it." Her lips dipped into the smallest frown. Almost undiscernible but it was there.

"Why?" I asked, because I was genuinely curious.

"Honestly?" Isabella finally looked at me.

I nodded while reminding her of her own words. "We agreed no lies."

"I wouldn't have invited half of the people in this room. And I would have chosen something more intimate." Her eyes bounced around again. "And more flowers. God, I'd have them on every surface."

"What's your favorite?"

"Flower? I don't think there's a type I don't love." She grinned, and it was the first honest expression I'd seen on her face. "This is just *too much*. But…"

"Our fathers," I finished for her, and the tension seemed to ease out of her shoulders as we laughed.

Various couples joined us on the floor as one song switched to another. And we got lost in each other. For a moment, we were just two ordinary people on our wedding day. At the same time, it felt like our first date. Which wasn't far from the truth. I learned that Isabella's heart really was made of gold. She wondered if I'd let her donate our shared finances and *her* time to charities. And she wanted to fill the house with fresh flowers from a garden she hoped to tend to herself.

Yes, it was true that the woman had a softness about her. But it was only skin deep. She wasn't afraid to put the work in. To get her hands dirty. The symbolism was there and it sure as fuck wasn't lost on me. My sour mood had exponentially lifted as I envisioned our future together. The potential behind this union my father had orchestrated.

And then the gun discharged.

I grabbed Isabella, tugged her towards our table, and flipped it over while my men moved quickly to surround us.

"That motherfucker." Rick was at my back in seconds.

"You see the shooter?"

"Didn't need to. Caelan fucking O'Reilly," he hissed the name as my hand tightened on Isabella.

Caelan was the president of the Rale Bulgarians MC. The fuckers liked to hang out on the other side of the bridge but had been sniffing around Philly and New York. Metro and I had no clue what they wanted. However, if they had something to do with this, they were all dead. I didn't have many interactions with the man, but this seemed off. Caelan didn't choose random violence. And he didn't hide. The sick bastard liked to look you in the face when he slit your throat. And I respected that. But this, if it really was him, would be the end of the fucker. And his club.

"Mario," Isabella called out my name, my glare flicking in her direction before landing on the pool of red forming around her.

CHAPTER 4

ISABELLA

The panicked look on Mario's face was endearing until it morphed into that of a madman. He started barking orders, and before I knew it, I was surrounded by his men, being rushed from the room and ushered into the back of a limo.

His phone started ringing the moment he lowered himself beside me. I could read the indecision on his face. I'd expected him to take the call, was shocked when he didn't. His attention remained firmly on me and my stomach.

"Stop, Mario, stop." I hissed out as his hands tore open my dress and he began inspecting my wound. "Ouch."

He froze when his glare landed on the glass shard embedded in my skin. He'd flipped the table over so quickly he'd shattered the wine glass he'd been so adamant about me having.

"It's not all that deep." He sat back in his seat and reached for my hand. "The family doctor will meet us at my penthouse."

"I'm fine, really. It's nothing more than a little blood." His phone started ringing again, cutting into my whispered words. "I'm used to it."

23

Was it her? The woman from outside the church?

Grabbing the towel from Mario's hand, I held it to my side and pivoted my body towards the window. "You can answer it. I'm fine." I refused to look at him even as I felt his eyes on me.

The limo pulled into an underground parking lot beneath the skyrise that served as the hub for the entire Agostino empire. We were immediately surrounded again as Mario lifted me from my seat and carried me inside. The elevator shot to the highest floor, landing us in a penthouse before a man with a medical bag ushered us to a bedroom.

I was placed on the bed, and the doctor opened his bag. Mario's phone blared throughout the room once again. My husband's face gave him away. He knew who it was, the device clutched in one hand as the older gentleman began to examine me.

"The wound appears to be superficial. Do you normally bleed like this? Are you hemophilic?"

I shook my head. "No. Von Willebrand disease." Both the doctor and Mario seemed surprised. "I got it from my mother. She died in childbirth."

"Good to know for when you prepare to have children. A few quick sutures should stem the bleeding. Then we'll give you some fluids and let you rest." The doctor's hands were cold as he continued to probe my abdomen.

"Will she need a transfusion?" Mario held up the blood-drenched towel I'd pinned to my side, his expression tense.

"Not at this time, no. Her coloring is good. She's warm to the touch and vitals are within normal range, considering the trauma her body has endured. Fluids should be sufficient. But we will keep a close eye on her." The doctor paused, his eyes flicking between us before landing on Mario again. "That said, Mr. Agostino, you should understand the severity of this disease…"

"I'm fine." I waved a dismissive hand. "Just don't cut me open anytime soon and we'll be good." I forced out a laugh, only to have it fall short.

"I have to…" Mario stepped to my side, but I couldn't look at him. "I'll be back shortly."

His words left me in a chokehold. He was leaving me. On our wedding night. This was not how things were supposed to go. He was supposed to take my virginity, hopefully get me pregnant, and pretend like I was the love of his life.

The moment he squeezed my shoulder, his mouth pulled tight. Would this always be my future? "You're safe. My men will be in the surveillance room off the kitchen, along with the men your father sent over."

"Okay." I refused to let my voice waver, even as I felt the sharp stab of the needle in my arm—the one in my chest cut far deeper anyway.

"All done," the doctor cooed, and when I looked up again, my husband was gone.

"Thank you." I nodded, and the old man patted my hand, a kind smile on his face as he saw himself out.

A few hours passed before I couldn't stand the silence anymore. So I pushed up from the bed and padded over to the bathroom, leaning on the vanity and staring at myself in the mirror while trying to determine if I had a right to be angry with a man I barely knew.

I understood what this marriage was. A contract, made between families and not the two people whose lives they held in the balance. But I'd told myself I was allowed *one night* to pretend.

Truth was I didn't know what my husband was doing right now. He should be hunting down whoever took it upon themselves to crash our wedding. But the butterflies in my stomach said he could be out searching for his lover.

I decided to push those negative thoughts aside and explore the penthouse instead. The decorations were sparse, simple, and in desperate need of a woman's touch.

Would I be that woman? It was sad to think I didn't have an answer to that question.

I found myself standing outside a door. I tugged it open and my husband's distinct scent immediately filled my nostrils. My gaze bounced around the room. The black silk sheets, black curtains, and white furniture screamed masculinity while the closet was filled with suits and clothing, all organized by color. It took me a second too long to realize what was missing.

Where were my things? They'd been shipped here a week prior to my arrival.

"Bells?" my father's voice called out, drawing my attention away from that question and towards the living room. I turned on my heel and headed in that direction. My father wrapped me in his arms and pulled me close the moment I was within reach. Then he kissed the top of my head like he always did.

Comfort. Safety. Happiness. It all hit me at once and I struggled to keep the tears at bay.

"I was so worried. But I knew Mario would take care of you." His chest rumbled with his deep baritone.

"The almost fatal wineglass." I grinned into his shirt, and we both laughed.

"Thankfully, no one was actually hit." This time, his chest lifted with a long sigh. "When I saw all that blood, I couldn't help but think—"

"Don't. Don't do that." I knew he was picturing my mother, how he lost her so soon after they were married. "I'm okay."

He took a moment to collect himself, then kissed my head again. "I have a few things to discuss with your *husband.*" His mouth dropped when he said that last word, like it tasted bitter on his tongue.

"He's not here," I said, and watched my father's brows pinch together.

"But his security is," he countered, and as if on cue, a man stepped out from the room just off the kitchen. "Where is he?"

"Mr. Agostino had business to attend to. He left Mrs. Agostino in my care and under my protection." The man was tall, wide, and bald. His attention drifted from my father and refocused on me. "I didn't want to disturb you while you were resting, ma'am. My name is Mark. I will be your personal security detail."

"Where. Is. Her. Husband?" My father was gone and in his place was *il capo*.

"On. Business," Mark stated simply, his expression stoic. Unfazed. "Now, Mrs. Agostino, if you're agreeable, I would like to connect in the morning to discuss any upcoming plans or outings. It's not a problem if we need to adjust, but I like to be as prepared as possible, especially until… the events of this evening have been appropriately handled."

"Plans?"

"Yes, ma'am. Mr. Agostino wants you to feel at home here. Decorate to your liking and so on."

"Oh, okay." I glanced between Mark and my father. "Thank you. Well, I am quite tired and I am sure you two have business to discuss."

Mark nodded as I hugged my father and wandered back down the hallway towards the bedroom that clearly didn't belong to my husband. The closet called to me. Dread settled in my stomach as my fingers gripped the handle, opened the door, and I dropped to my knees. The tears I'd tried so hard to hold back came freely. My arms wrapped protectively around my legs as I curled into a ball. My sobs rattled my body and I purged the anger mixed with sadness until nothing was left.

I pushed to my feet, my fingers dancing over the various fabrics hung along the far wall. My clothes were neatly arranged in the closet of the guest bedroom. The simple dress slipped off my shoulders, and I left it to pool on the floor as I changed into a pair of satin pajamas. Then I pulled back the covers and slid into the cold bed. Alone.

The pain radiating from my side as well as my heart left me to toss and turn all night, my dreams plagued by nightmares and memories alike. And when I rose the next morning, I realized my husband still wasn't home.

I headed into the kitchen when the daylight finally crept through the curtains, prepared to make myself a small breakfast, hoping it would settle my stomach. If my husband wanted me to turn this house into a home, then I would transform it from a bachelor pad to a place worthy of raising a family. Even if it was in a New York high-rise and nothing like the several acres of land I'd always dreamed of having.

I spent a summer in Texas at a ranch when I was a teenager. And fell in love with the scenery, the feel of dirt under my nails, and most of all, the horses. There was just something about the animals that called to me. A quiet peacefulness that seemed to soothe those who needed it the most. Especially children who found it hard to connect with others.

I froze when my gaze landed on an older woman presently milling about the kitchen. She paused to look up at the sound of my approach. "Mrs. Agostino, how nice to meet you." Strong arms wrapped around my waist and pulled me against her. I softened in her embrace, the kind only a mother could give you. "Sit. I'm just making breakfast. Would you like a coffee?"

"Yes, plea—"

"Frances, can I have a—" Mark stopped short, dipping his chin in greeting. "Good morning, ma'am."

"Please. Both of you. Just call me Isabella."

They shared a glance before Frances set a mug of coffee in front of me. I didn't miss how it was served to my liking without me having to verbalize it.

"Let me know when you'd like to review your plans," Mark said just as the front door opened.

"Frances! A coffee, please—" Mario paused in his tracks the moment his eyes landed on me. "Good morning."

Frances deposited another coffee on the counter, then disappeared with Mark. And suddenly I felt vulnerable in front of this man, my husband. I swallowed roughly, unsure of what to say.

"Did you sleep well?" Mario was wearing the same clothes he'd worn to the ceremony and looked like he hadn't slept. "I apologize for being gone so long. We had a lead I needed to hunt down…"

An honest smile graced my lips. I thought he'd been with another woman—*with her*. Instead, he'd been off trying to find the person—or people—who'd ruined our wedding day. We drank our coffee in silence until he asked if I'd explored the house. Asked what I had planned for it.

"Mark and I were about to review the plans for today."

"Good. Tonight, we'll have dinner. Just you and me." That *demand* made me smile. "Have fun but be safe." He wanted to please me after all.

Mario pulled me into an awkward hug. At the wedding, we'd seemed to have this comfortable connection. And now we were practically strangers. His grip tightened and I melted against him, letting the stress lift off my shoulders.

And then I smelled it. The subtle whiff of perfume clinging to his skin and flitting through the air. I stiffened and I could tell he felt it as he pulled away from me. Standing a couple inches shorter, I stared at his neck… and the red lipstick peppering his collar.

He had been with a woman.

"Well, have a good day." I shrugged him loose, my tone clearly annoyed.

Mario faltered at my darkened tone.

Mark walked back into the room and I let him know that I was ready to connect with him. Mario and Mark stepped to the side for a hushed conversation as I finished my coffee. And then I saw Mark tap his own neck. Mario shifted before his eyes drifted in my direction.

I held his gaze, refusing to falter. He gave me a weak smile and left the room as I turned to Mark and listed off all the places I would like to go. Furniture stores, an art gallery, a few tourist attractions, and a large florist.

Mark headed off to gather the men and have the car readied. While I remained rooted to the spot for a moment, unsure if I should say something to my husband before I left. Only to decide I wouldn't be afraid in my own home.

I could hear him moving about the bathroom in *his* bedroom. So I made my way there, stepped over the threshold, and closed the door behind me. I watched him undress, his muscles rippling with the movement, every surface toned. There wasn't a single part of him that wasn't perfectly sculpted and hard. Even his dick, which was standing tall against his lower abdomen. It was large, much like his towering stature.

He approached me, slowly. I didn't move, unable to look away. Until I caught the hint of her perfume again, and I took notice of the recognizable lipstick marks curling around his cock. And my rage and disgust resurfaced. I reached out a steady hand, wrapped it around him, and glided my palm up and down a few times.

"A fan of red, I see?"

CHAPTER 5

MARIO

I watched the deep red soak through the pure white of Isabella's dress, heard the sound of Fina's voice calling out to me while the sulfuric scent of gunpowder clung to the air.

Put it all together and I was ready to snap.

I'd left my security with Isabella while I met up with Rick back at the venue. We busied ourselves reviewing grainy surveillance video and setting up hourly check-ins with my men. It was late by the time we were done, and I just wanted to crawl into my bed and deflower my wife.

My dick twitched at the thought. Frances had set up the spare room until my new bride was comfortable with the sleeping arrangements. I wasn't sure if she'd be ready on her first night. Even if all I'd wanted to do was tear that dress from her body and take her in front of everyone.

I already had a splitting headache, and the constant ringing of my phone wasn't helping. I didn't have to answer to know who it was. She was calling… again. Only one person would have the nerve to be so persistent.

"Fina," I answered on an exasperated sigh.

"M-Mario," she sobbed. "He… he… My father is going to marry m-me off."

My knuckles turned white as my grip tightened around the steering wheel. "To whom?"

"He didn't say. We have to go… Please, let's run—"

I cut in before she could finish her rambling. "Fina, I'm married. We're—"

"Don't say it. Please. Not tonight. I hate the idea of you being with her. I-I need you," she was swallowing back her cries, nearly choking when she spoke. I took a deep breath, ready to tell her to go to bed, when her next words gave me pause. "I'd rather die than be without you."

She wouldn't.

She was rambling now, going on and on about how she couldn't live without me. It was the conviction in her voice that had me driving towards her house. The pain in her eyes that had me pulling her into my arms the moment I stepped through her front door. And when she dropped to her knees and took my cock in her mouth, it was that final release that had me abandoning my wife on our wedding night.

Isabella deserved a better man than I could ever be. I'd fucked Fina's throat, her pussy, and her mouth again. And then drowned myself in enough alcohol to forget all about it.

I sabella was sipping coffee when I stumbled into my—*our*—kitchen the following morning. She was chatting with Mark and Frances, who seemed to be enjoying her company. As if they too had fallen for her charms. And now I was an outsider in my own home. Or maybe it was just the guilt that left me feeling out of sorts.

I should have headed right to my bedroom to wash off my betrayal and change into some clean clothes, but something about my new bride gave me pause. The disgust I had for my actions aside, she was beautiful. The hungry look as she perused my body had my dick hardening all over again… despite the attention it had received just a few hours ago.

She seemed happy at the mention of dinner, pleased with my affections. Until something suddenly flared to life inside her. Her expression became closed off, and she went rigid in my arms.

Mark came back in the room—I hadn't even seen him step out —while Isabella began to put distance between us. As he pulled me aside to speak, he tapped his throat. Rubbing the spot on my own neck, I saw the lipstick now staining my fingertips.

Fuck.

I didn't bother to make excuses as I pivoted on my heel in need of a shower. The last thing I expected was for my new bride to follow me into the bathroom. For her to close the door behind her and approach me with a dark expression. When her hand began stroking my dick, I felt my knees nearly buckle beneath her grip.

"A fan of red, I see?"

The odd question hit me like a bucket of ice water. My eyes flicked down and that's when I saw it. Fina's preferred shade of red lipstick and the perfect rings it made around my cock. I'd been such a mess when I left. Sated. Spent. And yet so riddled with a stabbing sensation in my chest I hadn't bothered to shower. I'd come home to my new wife with another woman's scent still lingering on my skin. And like the sick bastard I was, if Isabella had taken things further, I would've fucked her too.

The door didn't slam, not like the fits Fina was known to throw. Instead, the soft click echoed worse than a gunshot before Isabella's heels clicked slowly down the hallway and the front door closed a moment later. And I stood there in my bathroom, my pants around my ankles, covered in my mistress's love bites, and wondered what the fuck I was going to do.

I'd fucked up and had no idea how to make it right.

Fina was relentless in her efforts to contact me over the next few weeks while I did my best to ignore her existence. Despite this, my marriage remained in name only. Isabella and I hadn't spoken since the incident in the bathroom. I did what was expected of me and she fulfilled her every obligation as a wife— except for those that required us sharing a bedroom. Which meant I only saw her in passing. Or at the few events we'd attend to save face with *il famiglia*.

My wife would smile and chat with all the appropriate guests. She would cling to my arm and charm the crowd, expressing her newfound love for our city. She would discuss her favorite art galleries and tourist spots and tell them all how excited she was to decorate our home. And then she'd turn her dazzling smile my way and wait for me to add to the conversation. I kept things brief, enjoying the sound of her voice far more than my own.

People were drawn to Isabella and it wasn't long before she became fast friends with several of the women from the most influential families in the city. Including those outside our usual circles and those who stayed on the right side of the law. She'd agreed to luncheons, committees, and benefits in the name of giving back. Like I said, the woman had a heart of fucking gold. Whereas mine was black, matching the darkness of the sky on the night I cheated on her.

As soon as these events would conclude, I would see the shift in Isabella. She would drop the mask along with her smile and we'd ride home in silence. File into the house and go our separate ways. But not before she would place a soft kiss on my cheek and offer me a whispered *goodnight*.

Then she would disappear into her bedroom, and I would crawl into some hole and get drunk. I would often find myself standing outside her door, swaying a bit as my brain and cock battled over whether I should barge in and take her. Something always kept me from crossing that threshold though. And eventually I'd turn around, jack off in the shower, and debate calling Fina until I drank myself to sleep.

It was the same thing. Every night. Rinse and repeat. And part of me knew I only had myself to blame.

"What do you mean the truck is missing?"

Rick shrugged and I was ready to take all my pent-up aggression out on him.

"That was almost a half a million dollars…"

"I got feelers out. Think we have a lead."

Motherfucker should've started with that.

"And?"

Instead of responding, Rick motioned for me to follow him to the car, where my men were already waiting. I slid into the back seat. Rick jumped in after me and slammed the door shut. It wasn't until we pulled away from the curb that he started talking.

Apparently, the Russians were less than pleased with the shift in power. I was a threat to them. So a few guys left their homeland and headed to the States, looking to make waves and move up the ladder by hitting my shipments.

The car came to a stop at an abandoned mill on the outskirts of the city. "What're we waiting for?"

Several cars filled with my soldiers circled my own. A show of force as we waited. A few of my men piled out, then stood armed and ready at my door.

"For the signal." Rick sat forward, looking out the window.

Before I could ask what he meant, a figure came running out of the mill, followed by one of my men. The guy looked up, spotted the caravan of cars, stumbled, and quickly hit the concrete. My door was open and I was charging for him before he could push back up to his feet again. I might have had an army of men but I liked doing my own dirty work. It reminded people what I was capable of… those in my ranks and those outside it.

"No touch me, *ital'yanskaya mraz'*."

My fist cracked against the fucker's jaw and sent blood raining down on the pavement. "What was that?" I punched him again. "Speak English, you fuck."

He kept mumbling in Russian. Truth was I didn't care what the fuck he had to say, what names he called me. What I did give a fuck about was finding the guy he was working for. A few more good blows to the ribs, and the bastard was hunched over and sniveling. It was the exact release I needed—as close as I was going to get until my wife finally forgave me and let me sink into that tight pussy of hers.

"Boss, we got it." The sound of my missing truck coming up behind us had me turning in that direction. "Four dead inside."

I returned my glare to the man curled up at my feet. "Who gave the order?"

The Russian spit at my shoes and I leaned forward to grip his face.

"I said. Who. Gave. The order?" Weak men were boring and I was done wasting my time on this one. "I guess I'll just have to tell Sergei all about the fucking rat he employed."

The eyes always told you what the tongue refused to say aloud. I'd been grasping at straws, curious if the *Bratva's* newest protégé was stupid enough to fuck with me. Sergei was a young kid, too big for the pants he wore. Barely a teenager and he thought he was tough enough to go toe-to-toe with the Italian mob.

And not just the mob, but with me. This was no doubt an unsanctioned rogue mission orchestrated by a kid looking to make a name for himself.

"Rick." I reached out an arm and waited until the cold metal was deposited on my open palm. My eyes flicked down and back up again as a slow grin curled my lips. "You've pissed your pants." It was my only warning before I pried open the Russian's mouth and got a firm grip on his tongue with the pliers. "There's only one way to silence a rat. *Do svidaniya, cagna.*"

My blade sliced through the lump of meat like I was a butcher preparing your mother's Sunday roast at the corner deli before his screams died off into a wet gurgle. Blood sprayed across the front of my suit and peppered my shoes as I dropped the worthless pile of shit back onto the concrete and ordered my men to clean it up.

"Send a message to our friends in Russia. Tell 'em their new little dog is off his leash," I grunted as I pulled a handkerchief from my pocket and used it to wipe off my hands.

I didn't need more enemies knocking at my front door. My father would want to start a war, but that didn't make sense. Not now. Not when we were just making headway. My message would get back to Russia and they'd call Sergei home. Or kill him.

Either way, the *Bratva* as a whole wasn't my problem. Vultures like Sergei always circled the air until they found their prey. I wasn't blind to what the fucker was looking to do. He wanted what my family had built. Thing was, he would have to pry it from my cold, dead hands first. And that wasn't happening today.

No, today, I needed to get home to my fucking wife. And try to climb out of the fucking hole I'd dug myself into.

"He's not up yet. Would you like me to get him?"

The sound of Isabella's voice lured me farther down the hallway, while my best friend's reply had me pausing in my tracks and clenching my fists at my sides. It took everything in me to not punch him in the face.

"Marriage looks good on you. You're glowing."

"Oh, stop. You're always such a charmer, Rick." She laughed, but it was forced as I watched her put distance between them.

The tight set of her shoulders and the fake smile plastered on her face left me curious. Whenever we were together, Isabella seemed to only engage with Rick when he directed a question her way. She'd smile and laugh before quickly moving on. Now that they were alone, she was tense and appeared unnerved by his presence.

Why was that?

"There he is. Is your new wife wearing you down?" Rick barked out a laugh while slapping a palm against my back. "Isabella, you animal. He never sleeps late."

I wish I could tell my friend the truth. That I was too much of a bastard to touch my wife. That as much as I dreamed of burying myself deep inside her, I hadn't. That it was overindulgence that kept me in bed late into the morning.

"Don't speak to her like that," I grunted. Isabella offered me a tight smile in return. "Office."

Rick chuckled as he trailed in behind me. He closed the door before turning to me with a slick grin on his face. "It's always the quiet ones, eh?"

I ignored his comment, my eyes flicking over to the bar cart. But it was far too early for me to be drinking again. At least in shared company. I'd slept for fuck all once again and was running ragged with everything that needed my attention.

"Got news," Rick hummed as I dropped into my chair. My ears perked up. "Caelan is denying it."

"And we believe him?"

"He wants a sit down with you. Also—" Rick paused, and I urged him to continue with a flick of my wrist. "Moretti's been whispering to anyone willing to listen, claiming it wasn't the MC. That it was him who called the hit on you."

Anthony-fucking-Moretti. The fucking bastard.

He hated the fact that his father was a fucking leech while mine ran the city. He'd wanted everything I had but refused to put the work in to get it.

"He's attending the gala tonight," I mentioned aloud.

Isabella had given me the guest list. It varied from the most prominent figures in our circle to the elite of New York. She'd stepped in to partner with one of the other wives in *il famiglia*, turning a small affair into a large benefit. She'd used every one of her contacts to make sure the night would be a huge success.

"Thinking what I'm thinking?" Rick was the first person to get an honest smile out of me in weeks. I nodded and he grinned. "I'll see you tonight then."

By the time Mark interrupted me in my office several hours later, I was late. I moved fast to shower and dress in my tux.

Isabella was already at the event with her father and his security. This was his last obligation before he headed back to Sicily.

My driver took us to my hotel, my biggest investment to date. Mark rode in the front while more men followed behind us. I wasn't taking any chances. Moretti was in attendance tonight, and if he tried to pull anything, I'd fucking kill him.

I didn't care how many people were there to witness it.

News reporters lingered outside, taking pictures of various guests and shouting questions to anyone who even glanced in their direction. My affiliation with the mob wasn't a secret; proving it was a different story altogether. My wife was a welcomed distraction, though. People loved her and her big heart.

The moment I stepped foot in the ballroom, everything else faded away. And all I saw was her. Isabella's black gown was tight and simple. Tasteful, while a slight dip in the neckline revealed her perky breasts. The high slit at her thigh made me want to throw that leg over my shoulder and taste her pussy.

"Excuse me." She dipped her chin in a polite apology before stepping away from her crowd of admirers. She pulled me in for a hug, clinging to my arm as I kissed her head.

"Dance with me?"

She smiled and nodded as I guided her to the dance floor.

Couples formed a circle around us to watch as one song trickled into two. I couldn't take my eyes off her. She was so beautiful with a softness that I craved. To the outside looking in, we appeared the perfect couple. I knew better than most that things weren't always as they seemed.

My marriage was in shambles.

I cleared my throat, drawing her attention to my face. "Is there anything you can't do? The event... the home you've made us... and you look beautiful."

Isabella didn't say anything for a while, just held onto me as we swayed. "I want a family." Her words broke the silence and rooted me to the spot. "I am well aware of what is expected of me as your wife. I've always known I wouldn't get fidelity, but I want a family."

"Isabella, I'm—"

"Save it, Mario." She urged me to start dancing again. "I'm not naïve. I know men like you have certain needs… Needs that you aren't fulfilling with me. But I can't build a family on my own, and I'm assuming you don't want me to seek comfort elsewhere."

"Fuck no." Rage took over at the mere thought of someone else touching her. "I will give you a family."

"Thank you. Please excuse me." Before I could say anything else, she was walking off in the opposite direction and climbing the few steps to the center platform. "Welcome, everyone."

The crowd went silent, all attention on her.

"Such a beautiful wife, Mario. Sorry I missed the opportunity to offer my congratulations at your wedding."

I turned my glare on Anthony Moretti and watched him twitch with discomfort. "You weren't on the guest list? Must've *missed that*." My palms itched to put a bullet between his eyes.

"Oh. Well, hello." Anthony directed his smirk over my shoulder, and I turned before I could stop myself.

"Fina."

The sound of clapping had me refocusing on my wife as she opened a piece of paper and read the contents aloud, announcing the five million dollars they'd garnered in donations. Serafina stood at my back, begging to stand at my side, while men and women came in waves to shake my hand and congratulate me on my wife's accomplishments. Politicians, CEOs, and other powerful men who normally kept their distance.

Until my wife.

Isabella was our key to branching out, to making connections outside of back alleys and corrupt business deals. They flocked to her, and she trapped them in her orbit.

"Wow. Congrats." Fina tossed back her champagne and grabbed another from a passing waiter.

I ignored her, my eyes glued to Isabella as she descended the podium.

She wanted a family. And I wanted to give her one. Just the thought got me hard.

"*Non lo meriti, stronza.*" Suddenly Fina was at my side, snarling at my wife's approach. "*Lui è mio.*"

I could smell the booze radiating off her and knew she was about to do something stupid. Gripping up her arm, I pulled her from the room and all but threw her into the service hallway. "Get. Out," I hissed while staff scattered in various directions. "What the fuck do you think you're doing?"

"I've missed you." Fina's glassy eyes couldn't focus on any one thing, and her palms pressed into my chest to keep her upright. "You've been so busy with your *new wife* you can't answer my calls? Come to see me? I miss you." She flicked open my zipper and reached inside before I could stop her, her movements far too quick for someone so seemingly inebriated. My dick was half-hard and her smile was devious.

If only she knew it wasn't for her.

There was a time when I thought I could settle down with Fina. Make her my wife, have a family. Meeting Isabella had changed all that. I couldn't imagine myself with anyone else now.

I was so stunned by that admission, I didn't realize what was happening until Fina was on her knees, wrapping her lips around my cock. "No." I wrenched my hands through her hair and tried pulling her off me. "Fina, enough."

"I believe he's back here." Anthony Moretti's voice drew closer before the door flew open. "Oh. No." Anthony gasped, covering his mouth with a hand but I could see his lips curling into a grin. "Mario, how could you?"

He was fucking dead.

"The senator and his wife would like a word," Isabella called out from behind him, her tone dry and her expression cold. She finally glanced at Fina, who had stopped sucking my dick, before adding, "When you're done." Then she pivoted on her heel in a flurry of black lace with Anthony gloating behind her.

Fina moaned around me, but it didn't matter. My dick was about as interested as I was. I tucked myself back into my pants and left her on her knees.

How the fuck did I let that happen?

I stalked out the door, shoving Anthony aside as I went in search of my wife. When I spotted her by the back bar, I stormed that way.

"There he is. Mario, let me introduce you to Senator Richard Gaines." Isabella smiled—tight and forced. "Richard, this is my husband, Mario."

She was hurt. And once again, it was because of me.

"That sounds lovely. Let's schedule lunch. You and Mario can discuss business, and I can speak with your wife about the next gala."

We said our goodbyes and I wrapped Isabella in my arms.

She shrugged out of my hold before turning to Mark. "I'm ready to head home."

He nodded and went in search of our driver.

"Papa, thank you for coming." Isabella pulled her father into a hug. He returned the gesture while pinning me with a glare. Only those closest to her could recognize her anger. Her pain.

Could see what I'd done to her.

"A moment of your time, please, Mario." He motioned for me to follow him to a darkened corner. "What the fuck did you do?"

"I've warned you to watch that tone, Michele."

"And I warned you not to hurt my fucking daughter. You think I don't have eyes on her? That I can't read her pain through those forced smiles?" He paused, crossing his arms over his chest. "My men told me about your whore... here, at my daughter's event. On her fucking knees for you in the back room, making a mockery of my sweet Isabella."

"Isabella, my wife, is no longer your concern. I control my household, how I—"

He interrupted me with angry laughter. "Control? You can't even control your dick around a whore who doesn't know her fucking place. Because of *my daughter,* you just met with a fucking senator. Because of her, you will be the most powerful *capo* in the States. Yet you fucking disrespect her?"

"I won't fucking tell you again to watch how you—"

He shoved at my chest, forcing me back a step. "Watch how I talk to you? No, I'm watching how you treat my daughter. And it disgusts me."

"Then go the fuck back home."

"You're fucking dead." His arm shot out, his palm wrapping around my throat while his free hand cocked into a fist. I shrugged him loose and raised my own. Until a blur of black lace shoved between us. We both froze as Isabella gripped our lapels, forcing our attention on her.

"You will *not* do this. Not here. Not ever." Her tone meant she wasn't to be trifled with. "Papa, I'm fine. You raised me right. I can take care of myself because of you. Go home and be safe."

"But... he..."

She smiled at him. "I've got this. He's my husband. I love you and I thank you for coming. I'm going to miss you."

He pulled her in for a tight hug, glaring at me over her shoulder.

"Call when you're home safe. Now, can we go?" She lifted a challenging brow at me, and I nodded.

This woman was a fucking force.

She'd stepped into the middle of a fight and didn't flinch.

Coaxing us to do her bidding without having to spill blood. I needed to figure out how to apologize. To make it better.

My men surrounded the limo parked at the curb out front and Isabella refused my offer to help her inside.

It wasn't until we were merging with the traffic that I finally had the balls to speak up. "Isabella, I—"

"I know you have a past. And I know neither of us had a choice in this." She slowly turned from the window, pinning me with her fiery glare. "As you've seen firsthand, I'm an asset. I can help you build an empire unlike anything this city has ever seen before."

"And?" I didn't like where this was headed.

"*And* if you want to keep fostering those relationships, you will do something for me." Her tongue flitted across her full lips. "You know I want a family—something you've already agreed to give me. That said, I have conditions. While we're trying, I will be your only focus. No other woman may have your… *attention* until I have what I want."

"Now, look…"

"One last thing." She pivoted in my direction, and everything about her body language told me this was nonnegotiable. "When I *am* pregnant, I will continue to support you as long as you do not seek out *that* woman. Anyone else. But not her. Physical cheating is one thing… but emotional cheating is something else entirely. It's unforgivable and won't be tolerated."

The car came to a stop inside the parking garage, and Isabella opened the door without another word. She moved gracefully as my men surrounded her approach to the elevator.

What the fuck?

How was I supposed to tell her that she was all I'd wanted? That she was all I could think about? That all I wanted to do was fuck her —consume her—since the moment she walked down that aisle.

First, I needed to shower. Second, I needed to destroy that fucking pussy. Show my wife just how much I fucking owned her.

The gala was even more successful than I imagined. I'd been fortunate because the senator's wife, Miranda, was an asset and turning into a good friend. I'd met her at a planning event for the new homeless shelter they were funding. Since then, we'd talked almost daily. Funny enough, I learned that her family was from Mexico and had just as dark of connections as I did. We were two peas in a pod, ensuring our husbands became powerful.

Most of my giving back was for me, not for Mario. While it did reap him benefits, it was about more than that for me. I enjoyed talking to those less fortunate than my family, showing them kindness, and seeing their faces light up. There was no mistaking their gratitude. I'd been born into wealth but that didn't mean my entire world glittered like gold. My desperation for a place to fit in—to be accepted—had brought me there.

And each day, it filled a different hole in my heart.

Until the night was ruined and reality came slamming back down around me again.

Anthony Moretti had no moral compass and was unable to stand in a room of men and earn their respect. I had no idea how he afforded the cost of the plate to attend. But that wasn't my business. As soon as he heard me calling out for Mario, he smiled at Miranda and whisked me away. My every nerve ending told me that his version of kindness had an ulterior motive.

And I'd been right.

I'd perfected the ice queen persona for the public and offered the same to my husband. The image of *that woman* on her knees pleasuring him wasn't something I'd ever forget. I wanted to feel bad for her—I really did. But no one felt bad for me. She didn't care that she was stealing my husband from me. The lonely virgin wife, locked away in her penthouse castle.

God, it was such a sad joke.

Draping my dress over one of my new armchairs, I walked into the bathroom. Naked. There was no one around to see me anyway. The scent of fresh flowers welcomed me as I turned on the hot water and allowed it to fill the tub. My body was riddled with tension and the urge to vomit had been present through most of the ride home. Thankfully, it'd subsided the moment I got away from *him*. The stress of my marriage, the gala, and finding a place for myself in the city was weighing me down. A lavender-scented bath was just what I needed.

Mario hadn't stopped me from walking away from him when we arrived home. So I retreated to my room when I heard the clatter of his decanter in the kitchen. A drink before deciding what to do about my ultimatum, I had no doubt.

I slipped into the hot water, and the soft scent immediately calmed my nerves. The warmth loosened my tense muscles, and soon I felt myself relax. I closed my eyes and nearly fell asleep before the sound of glass shattering down the hall had me shooting upright.

What the hell was going on?

My first thought was: *They'd found me. They were back.* And suddenly I was catapulted back in time.

My heart was pounding as I curled up inside the pantry. The gunshots had alerted us that someone had broken into the compound, and the family chef quickly shoved me through the closest door and covered me with boxes.

"Your father isn't home, miss. If they're here, it's because they want you," she said, and then darted away just as someone entered the kitchen.

I pressed one eye against the small crack in the door and watched three armed men kill her. They didn't hesitate. She was nothing to them.

"I thought you said she was here," one grunted while the other sent everything on the counter crashing to the floor.

The shattering of glass made me jump and I closed my eyes, begging my breaths to slow. My heart was hammering out of my chest as they ransacked the kitchen while laughing amongst themselves. When my lashes fluttered open again, the dimming of light caught my attention.

"Hello, beautiful," one of the men whispered, his head lowered to the crack and an eye peering directly at me.

I'd been found.

Shaking myself from my thoughts and lifting the plug, I let the tub drain and grabbed a robe. The warm water slid down my leg as I quickly but silently moved towards the noise. It was coming from Mario's room. I could hear him muttering to himself. Pushing the door open, I watched him pace back and forth. He was dripping wet, naked, fresh from the shower.

"What the fuck? Just fucking do it. Go. Right now." He tugged on his damp hair before swiping another bottle from his dresser.

It shattered against the wall and my heart went along with it. I'd told him he couldn't see her and now he was battling with himself to go to her. I quickly turned around, ready to lock myself away in my room again.

"She's your fucking wife. Take her. Just fucking show her you want her," he continued muttering to himself. "She hates you. Fucking hates you."

A sane woman would've closed the door and retreated. Instead, I wanted us to have this moment. I wanted him to take me, indulge in the release we both needed. So I shoved the door open with more force than necessary. It bounced against the wall, and my husband tensed as I stepped inside. Water ran down his thick muscles, pulling towards his waist.

His cock instantly hardened and his steel-blue eyes seemed to glow in the dimly lit room. He followed the path of my tongue as I traced my lip, indecision now gone as I dropped my robe from my shoulders. His eyes turned hungry while my steps pulled me towards him.

"Wait."

I froze and watched Mario step over the glass littering the floor. Then he tugged me into his arms and draped me over the bed. He didn't move. Just looked down at me, almost as if he were trying to etch me into his memory. He hadn't kissed me since our wedding day. And when our lips finally did meet again, it was blissful. I lost myself to the feel of his hand roaming all over my body. Plucking, kneading, and searching as I melted beneath him.

"Mario, please," I begged.

He didn't need to be told twice. He slid down my body and buried his face between my thighs, and I instantly cried out in shock. He tasted and explored my folds, as I lost my composure. I screamed his name while my husband drew one orgasm after another from me. In the back of my head, I still pictured her lipstick on him. I could see her on her knees for him.

I shook my head and swallowed back my anger as I tried to stay in the moment.

Mario raised himself onto his elbows while stroking his hardened length. He was ready to take his bride, finally deflower her. But after weeks and weeks of everything he put me through, I no longer wanted to make it easy for him.

The man had broken my heart. Scooped me into his arms, made me believe all his lies, and then made a mockery of me. This arrangement wasn't something I could change, but I could control how I handled it.

"No." I scooted up the bed and rested my back against his headboard. "I need more." I parted my thighs and motioned for him to continue with his mouth.

On his arm and in his bed, I'd own him. In some form or another. If he wanted what I could do for him, my husband needed to show me what he could do for me first.

"Yes." I closed my eyes, holding his head where I needed him most. Once. Twice. Three times. I lost count before my eyes fluttered open again.

"Better?" he asked, and I nodded. "Now. It's my turn."

My breaths came out in short pants at the thought of having to return the favor. As much as I wanted this, I wasn't sure I was ready for… *that.*

Mario tugged me down the bed and onto my back before climbing between my spread legs. His tip pushed at my opening, and I closed my eyes and gritted my teeth. The whispered sound of my name had me staring up at him in confusion.

"Don't look away. I want to see you." Then, soft and tender, Mario finally took my virginity. His hips moved slowly as I breathed through the slight pinch of pain. He kissed my tears away and thanked me over and over.

And then he apologized for not doing this the first night.

When he tensed and came inside me, I didn't know how to feel. I cuddled into Mario's side as he covered me with kisses while offering more words of appreciation. A moment of indecision passed through me as I wondered if I should return to my room. Before I could decide, he turned off the light and pulled me against him.

We lay there in silence for a few minutes until the sound of his heavy breaths told me sleep was near. I slid down to get comfortable, and something hard rubbed against my backside. I couldn't stop myself from pushing against him.

And then my husband took me again…

He spent the night and well into the early morning buried deep inside me. My body was exhausted, sated, and happy. I'd just closed my eyes when his strong arms wrapped around me.

"Fina." He sighed into my ear.

And my heart shattered into a million pieces before my guard dropped back into place—this time reinforced. This man deserved nothing from me. Hopefully tonight worked, and we'd taken the first steps to starting a family. Because the moment I was pregnant, I'd tell Mario I wanted to live somewhere else. I wanted a home, not a bachelor's apartment. A place that was mine. That was fit for a family. Where he'd only be welcomed when I said so.

I looked down at my husband and pulled free from his hold. "I fucking hate you," I whispered, slipping out of bed and closing the door behind me. Then I returned to my room to drown in my own misery.

CHAPTER 8

MARIO

I'd skipped the gym this morning, planning to stay in bed with my wife. But when I'd woken up, she was gone and her door was closed. I'd debated far longer than I care to admit whether I should kick it down and tell her she'd sleep in my room from now on.

Just thinking of her deliciously tight pussy had me wanting her again. The natural way she moved, the little noises she made, the looks she gave me... it was far better than I ever expected it to be. It was more than I could ever want. And she was mine.

I made my way into the kitchen where Frances was milling around. I glanced at the table and saw my coffee waiting for me. "You served breakfast already?"

Frances was bent over the sink, scrubbing pots. "Yes, Mrs. Agostino ate and left very early this morning."

She was gone? What the hell happened between us fucking all night and her fleeing in the morning?

"What did you do?" Frances's glare caught me off guard. "She wasn't herself."

"Where did they go?"

I left my car on the curb outside the museum, not planning to stay long. Then I stormed inside, ready for a fight when security went to stop me.

"Please let my husband through." To anyone else, Isabella's voice sounded welcoming. Kind. But I knew better. My wife was pissed. "Hello, darling."

Standing on a glacier buck-ass naked would've been warmer than her greeting. Isabella kissed my cheek and shrugged me loose when I tried to hold her against me. A group of women, including the senator's wife, stood at her back, smiling at our seemingly loving embrace. Except there wasn't anything loving between us right now. Mark loomed in the distance, watching our interaction. I waved him off and he stepped down another hallway to give us space. He paused for a moment longer than I liked before my glare had him moving again.

"Yes?" Isabella urged, while I was struck dumb by her beauty. "Mario? What did you need?"

I knew I needed to verbalize an answer but I was lost to the memory of how soft and tight her pussy was. The sound she'd made as she gasped for air, right before she came… How her eyes went round, her breath became erratic…

"Mario."

"You left this morning." *Idiot.*

"Yes." She nodded and I waited for her to continue. "I introduced you to Miranda the night of the gala. She invited me to meet the other members of the committee here." Isabella lifted an arm and gestured to the museum. "With her help, you will be one of the larger benefactors supporting the restoration program."

I had no idea what my wife was talking about, nor did I care at the moment. Isabella gestured for me to follow her as she led me towards a private corridor and behind a guarded door. Where various museum guests were milling about.

"Their restoration process is meticulous, tedious, but most of all… *costly*. But it will be worth it in the end." Isabella continued to guide me through a back entrance. "There will be a large party with several politicians and prominent men in attendance, all looking to thank you for your generous donation. It'll be the perfect opportunity to ask them to aid in *your cause*."

Smart. Beautiful. The perfect wife really. Except for the coldness and distance she was currently placing between us. We'd finally given in to our natural desires—the clear need we had for one another—and she was closing herself off to me again.

Even so, she remained hyperfocused on extending our reach. With political and prominent alliances, I'd have a different level of protection. Something no *capo* had before me. My father had been jailed many times over the years with only a handful of cops in his pocket. With everything Isabella was setting into motion, I'd be untouchable.

"If there's nothing else, I have work to do." Her tone was dismissive as she moved to turn her back on me.

I was about to grab her arm, stop her and demand she tell me what her problem was when a few of her friends flitted in our direction. And Isabella's mask firmly slammed back in place.

"I missed you too." She kissed me on the lips, and my arms automatically wrapped around her waist and held her tight. Her body was tense, rigid beneath my touch, until her friends began gushing behind us. And Isabella turned our little embrace into an encore. For their benefit, not ours.

"Oh! Newlyweds!" Someone giggled.

Isabella pulled away from me. "See you at home, Mario." She forced a grin and then she was gone.

"Mark," I barked out, stopping him from following her. "Where is she planning to go today?"

He ran down the list and told me her favorite place was a florist in midtown. They had some sort of exotic flowers she loved. My wife had interests, desires, plans that I was clueless about. I'd left her alone in a strange city, in a penthouse. For weeks. My men knew more about her than I did. So I decided to change that. To get my wife to fall in love with me.

The question was: how the fuck did I do that? Usually, when a woman fell for me, it was onto her knees. And I never stayed around long enough to help her back up.

~

Flowers. Romantic dinners. Designer dresses for all her events. None of it cracked my wife's icy exterior. The only exception was when she melted beneath me at night. She didn't turn down the sex. Sometimes she even sought it out. Our nights were heated, passionate, while our days remained frigid. And it was really starting to piss me off.

I was jealous, resentful, set on ruining my liver and drowning my sorrows in whiskey.

There was a tap on my open office door before Mark crossed the threshold. "Sir, you have a meeting with Metro."

I'd pulled him off Isabella's security detail—thanks to her little stunt and the newfound jealousy it instilled in me. I began questioning every glance they shared, every whispered conversation, every inconspicuous touch. She'd opened up to him and Frances, offering her real self to them while refusing to share that part of her with me. I wasn't too proud to admit, at least to myself, that I also did it to ignite that fire in her. To force her to come crawling to me and beg for me to change things back. Never in my life had I craved a woman's defiance as much as I did my wife's. And she wouldn't budge.

I nodded at Mark, and he quickly excused himself from my

office. I waited a few seconds before I pushed up from my desk and slowly followed him into the kitchen. Where Isabella was seated at the table laughing with Frances. From my vantage point, I could see that my wife's smile was genuine and so goddamn beautiful as the older woman seemed to be trying—unsuccessfully—to teach her how to bake.

"Mark!" she cooed and turned that smile on him. "You should try some!" She gestured to the mess of dough piled up in front of her.

He laughed as he swiped a bit of flour from her nose. "Not a chance in hell."

The three of them fell into another fit of laughter until I stepped from the hall and was met by varying reactions. My wife turned her back to me and I stared at the way her hair bounced with the movement. My glare green-eyed and fucking dangerous.

Frances and Mark had everything I wanted. *Her.*

Cold fucking shoulder. Tight, forced smiles. Silent seething. And outright dismissals. The woman refused to even thank me for the flowers that were scattered over every available surface.

And I was fucking done.

That authentic laughter was mine. Her happiness was mine. Our nights together proved how good we could be. The passion was fucking amazing.

I'd been home every night with her. I'd stopped answering Fina's calls and threw myself into my work. Only to have someone else given everything I'd wanted.

"Ow! Mario, what the hell?" Isabella hissed, as my grip tightened around her arm and I dragged her from the room. "Let me go!"

Any other time I would've grinned at the quick crumbling of her façade. I'd hated the woman who smiled for the cameras and mingled with politicians' wives. However, I loved this version of her. The real, raw Isabella. The hellcat.

I stormed through my bedroom door and tossed her onto the

bed. Before she could move, I pinned her down. She fought like hell. I'd let her get a few hits—enough to make me bleed. Then I grasped both of her hands in one of mine.

"Are you mad?"

"For you? Yes." I ground my erection into her. "Have you fucked him?"

Her body froze, and I could tell by her face she was appalled *and* confused. *She hadn't.* She hadn't had sex with anyone but me. However, that didn't ease the jealousy. Her eyes lit with fire, and I waited for the animal to claw free.

She leaned up on the mattress until we were nearly nose to nose. "What if I had? What if he fucked me better, harder, longer than you ever could?"

"Don't fucking push me, Bella." I growled, tugging her arms towards the headboard and forcing her head to drop back down.

"Oh, just like that." She rubbed her pussy against my raging hard-on and moaned. "Please… give me more, *Mark*."

I wasn't the type of man to abuse women. As much as I wanted to choke the fuck out of her, I breathed through my rage. Shoving her aside before standing over her and removing my coat. Her eyes lit up, having gotten the rise out of me she wanted. Then I recognized the fear as I pulled my gun from my shoulder holster. I quickly checked the chamber, ensuring it was loaded, and flicked off the safety. I glared at her for a moment longer before pivoting towards the door.

"You don't like it, do you?" she hissed, and I stopped with my hand on the knob. "Hearing me moan someone else's name? Like a knife to the heart, isn't it?"

She climbed off the bed and stormed towards me. Her small fists beat my chest and I stumbled back against the closest wall.

"Your wife! With another man! Someone she clearly prefers over you. I feel bad, you know. Poor Mario! How it must hurt!"

I nudged her towards the bed, and she screamed.

I could hear footsteps charging down the hall. "Fuck off. She's fine!" I called out, and they quickly retreated.

"I am far from fine, but what choice do I have?" Isabella composed herself and moved to the armchair by the bed. Suddenly poised. Calmer than I'd ever seen her before. "I care for Mark… the same as I do for Frances. They're my only two friends in *il famiglia*. The only people who truly understand what I have to endure in this life and silently comfort my pain. My loneliness. And you took that—him—from me."

I was at a loss for words, unsure where to take this conversation.

"The next time you moan another woman's name in your sleep, remember how much *this* hurt. Then again, at least this was all a lie. Because I don't feel for him like you do for *Fina*." She put extra emphasis on my former lover's name. And it all finally fell into place. It was never a dream I was having; it was a nightmare. My subconscious realized how much better off I was with Isabella by my side.

But instead of apologizing. Instead of telling her just that. Clarifying the simple misunderstanding, my anger took over…

"You got what you fucking wanted." I didn't raise my voice. I let my words alone inflict the damage. "I fucked you. Again and again. You wanted a family. As long as I'm not directly fucking her, I can do whatever the fuck I want in my sleep and not breach the terms of our little agreement. I don't see the problem here, other than your overly delicate disposition… it seems."

Her mouth opened and closed a few times before she rose to her feet and approached me. The smallest tear ran down her cheek, and I hated myself. At the same time, I was too much of a prick to apologize.

"Yes. You got what you wanted as well, haven't you? Now, I want a brownstone, with a small yard. That will be my home and you can bring your whores here. I've already found a property to my liking. Mark has the details."

"You think I'll just let you live separately? Run around with as many men as you please? Do what you want? Is that it?"

Her soft hand stroked my cheek. "What I want is a family. And it's clear you're incapable of giving me *yourself* to complete that picture. So, I'd like a home where I don't have to smell other women on my sheets, down the hall, or on my husband."

"I don't fucking care what you want." Truth was… I did care. I cared too damn much.

"I figured. Fina is perfect for you. Cold. Callous. Dangerous when it comes to what you're trying to achieve. And now you don't have to touch me. Congratulations, I'm pregnant."

And then she used my shock against me and slipped under my arm. The door closed behind her and her words would play on repeat in my head for days.

Congratulations, I'm pregnant.

Fina is perfect for you.

And I was too much of a bastard to tell her she was the only woman I wanted.

CHAPTER 9
ISABELLA

We'd barely spoken in weeks. I hated him.

That's a lie. I hated how much I wanted him. How he plagued my thoughts. How my body was so damn traitorous. How I sought comfort from him.

Maybe it was the baby. Maybe it was just the man himself. But I craved him at night. I'd crawl between the sheets or wait until he came to me. And we'd get lost in each other.

Then, the next morning, reality would seep in all over again. Mario was the head of the largest crime syndicate in the States, now that his father had retired. Which meant women flocked to him. The only solace I had was when Serafina showed me her cards.

Miranda and I had attended a luncheon for the board members of a nonprofit that helped illegal immigrants with the process of citizenship. With a strong focus on battered women with children. We'd spent the afternoon hashing out the details and signing documents. Together we would be able to support hundreds—maybe thousands—of women who weren't as fortunate as her and me. My father had money, and she'd caught the eye of a powerful man. In a way, we'd each gotten here on our own… with the means from the men around us. While this program was meant to aid those who didn't have that luxury.

Before we left, I stopped in the bathroom. I was high off the adrenaline of our most recent accomplishment. And then it was ruined. The woman who haunted my nightmares caught me alone. And weeks later, our interaction still agitated me.

The cat was out of the bag with my pregnancy. Miranda had wanted to toast to our success, and when I declined the bubbles, she knew. And she was far more excited than my husband seemed to be.

Doctors were scheduled, my father—after learning he was going to be a grandfather—prepared to fly back, and I was debating on decorating the third bedroom in the penthouse. However, I was hoping Mario would grant my request for a new home before I made the leap.

In public, we were the perfect couple. Behind closed doors was another story. Mark was suddenly back on my protection detail, which was the closest to a ceasefire as one could get. That didn't mean I was happy. True joy would come when and if Mario attended my appointments, helped me pick out paint colors for the nursery so that we could finally build a family—a home—together. Instead of strained apathy.

"He doesn't love you."

The comment had me looking up into the mirror while a familiar reflection glared back at me.

"And he never will. He only wants me."

I quickly dried my hands, ignoring her as I steeled my back-bone. Women like Serafina liked to see you sweat. It was how they fed their egos, made themselves feel superior, when deep down the fear of inadequacy ate them alive.

"That's interesting." I paused long enough to have her shifting with discomfort. "I was unaware you spoke for your capo. Hmm."

She flinched.

Good. Serafina knew that if any of this got back to Mario, their... "relationship" wouldn't matter. He'd kill her just to prove a point. No one spoke for him. Not even me.

"I have no need when the walls in your home speak loud enough for both of you." When I didn't give Serafina the reaction she wanted, she tried again. With a little more venom. "You do know I've fucked him in every room of the home I decorated, right? Every surface."

"Well, thankfully, I've redecorated." I shoved past her and stepped towards the exit. "It was a little too... quaint for my liking."

My indifference was getting to her. I'd wanted to ask so many questions, make so many accusations but I kept myself together.

"You may have your hooks in him now, but he'll come back to me. He always does." And there it was. "He always ends up back in my bed because I'm in his heart."

"We'll see." I smiled as I pushed through the bathroom door.

She hadn't even realized her mistake. The fact that she admitted Mario hadn't been with her.

∼

L ast night, Mario came home drunk off his ass. He had another woman's lipstick on him again… but it didn't hurt my heart as much as it did any of the times before. Because I knew it wasn't hers.

Maybe it was a little sick for me to be thinking that way. It was certainly dumb. But in this world, it was also normal. I'd never expected my husband to be faithful. Perhaps he'd love me in his own way. If this was my glance into the future, I had *hope*.

Mario had a telltale sign when he'd been with someone else. Normally he'd stumble past my door towards his own and the audible click of the lock would tell me the truth. This was different. Tonight, he stumbled directly into my room, damn near falling over. Without a word, he pulled the blanket down and collapsed on his side. Staring at my stomach as his hands lightly embraced it. His gaze was soft and his touch was tender while my eyes filled with tears.

A few moments later, he pushed himself up and stumbled back out again. Almost like the whole thing had been a dream.

I couldn't stop the stupid smile on my face the following day. Mark and Frances were already in the kitchen. My morning sickness had yet to diminish, and as soon as Mark saw me, he dumped his coffee down the drain. There was something about the scent of coffee and chicken that had the contents of my stomach making their way up.

It was sad when your bodyguard knew things your own husband didn't.

"Ready?" Mark asked. We had an early appointment scheduled, and he knew I hated being late.

"In a min—" My words were cut short by a sharp pain in my abdomen.

"Ma'am?" Frances stepped closer, but I waved her off.

"I'm okay. Anyway, yes, we can g—" This time the pain was crippling. My legs gave out and I collapsed against the counter. Mark was on me in a second, but it wasn't him I wanted. "Ma-Mario," I called out, even knowing he'd already left for the day. Then I felt the blood dripping between my thighs and onto the kitchen floor.

"Call Mario!" Frances shouted into the security room. "We're taking Mrs. Agostino to the hospital. Tell him it's the baby." She was back at my side in an instant.

Mark scooped me into his arms, darting towards the elevator.

"It hurts," I whimpered against his chest.

"I've got you. We-we've got you," he quickly corrected himself.

The doors closed behind us as another sharp pain shot through me, and I screamed. Frances grabbed my hand as Mark held me tighter. Until the elevator rocked and Mark stumbled into the wall.

"Fuck!"

The lights dimmed and an alarm blared while Frances started aggressively pressing at each of the buttons. "It's okay, ma'am. They'll get to us quickly," she assured me, her smile tightened by worry.

"*Fa male!*" I twisted my body and clutched my stomach as I tried to do what I could to alleviate the pain. Mark slowly slid to the ground and held me close to his chest. "Fran-Frances. Am I?"

Her eyes dropped to the pool of blood soaking into Mark's slacks.

The words were stuck in my throat. I couldn't bear to utter them aloud. I loved this baby so much already. I couldn't lose it.

"No, ma'am. No." Frances nodded and I could hear the determination in her voice.

Time seemed to stand still, and what could've been minutes also could've been hours. All I knew was that the pain was subsiding, but my blood smeared on the floor beneath us.

"*Oh, grazie a Dio!*" Frances cheered when the lights flickered back on and the elevator began to move again.

We all watched the numbers drop until we finally hit the ground floor. As soon as the doors opened, Mario and Rick appeared on the other side. At first, I noted a hint of concern on my husband's face, but it quickly morphed into rage. And instead of asking if I was all right, he glared at Mark's arms around me.

"My car is out front." Mario practically ripped me out of my bodyguard's grasp and took off through the lobby.

And in that moment, I could have sworn I felt my heart harden towards him forever. Any love I had for this man would die with my unborn child. If Mario Agostino didn't want a cold, murderous bitch in his home, then he'd better pray to the devil to let me keep my baby.

"That perfume doesn't suit you, by the way."

CHAPTER 10

MARIO

"I. Won't. Ask. Again." I gripped the son of a bitch by the face. His entire body was covered in blood and bruises, his feet and hands bound to the chair in front of me.

"Tell us!" Rick grunted from where he was positioned at my side.

"Who. Hired. You."

We'd found the shooter from my wedding. A no-name gun-for-hire without ties to anyone. Fucker was loyal to the highest bidder. Now he was staring down the barrel of my nine. And something told me he was wishing his aim wasn't shit. He should have killed me when he had the chance.

The door opened behind me before one of my men stormed into the room. "Boss, Caelan O'Reilly is on the line for you," he said, and I watched the guy in the chair flinch.

Interesting.

"Caelan." I grinned into the phone.

"We have a mutual problem—mine involves people spreading rumors about me," he grunted. "I promise on my unborn son's life that I didn't sanction that hit. It's an enemy trying to have you do their dirty work for them."

"And why should I believe you?"

"You have no reason to, outside of the fact I don't want a war with New York. I have enough of my own bullshit going on. My wife... my wife is pregnant and..." He sighed. "When I got word on a rival club gunning for me, I was too late to stop the hit. But I handled them."

"Who hired him?"

"He's already dead. I'll dump him at your door to prove it."

I stared at the bleeding man at my feet. "And what about the problem I have?"

"Enjoy it. I'll drop his boss off to you in less than twenty-four." The phone call ended, and while I appreciated Caelan's dedication, I still wanted this asshole to suffer. He hurt my wife.

I roared my anger into the soon-to-be dead man's face. Stabbing my long blade through his leg and smiling when he cried out in agony. "Time's. Up. Motherfucker." I dropped the phone and dove on him.

Left. Right. Left. I landed blow after blow until blood soaked my clothes and my knuckles tore open. I welcomed the pain, barely registering it until I stopped to grab the blade still sticking in his thigh. I yanked it free and pressed the edge against his throat.

"Nessuno fa male all amia famiglia." Then I sliced the fucker from ear to ear, and a burst of fresh, sanguine fluid coated my face. I glanced over my shoulder at Rick.

"You really believe O'Reilly?" he asked.

"I do," I said. He nodded and tossed me a towel as I stepped towards the shower.

There was conviction in his voice. And I'd heard the rumors of a new MC treading closer to New York. If Caelan dealt with them, it would save me time and money on dry cleaning. It would also save me the blood of my own men.

After I'd showered, I headed upstairs to my office at the back of the bar to get some work done. I downed some whiskey and rubbed at the ache settling behind my eyes.

"I need to talk to you, Mario."

Fucking Fina.

I sipped at my whiskey. It was far too early to be drinking again, but it was helping with the hangover. I'd fucked Mags—my bartender—until the early hours of the morning and then went home. Burying my dick inside her and draining my balls left me feeling worse than when I'd started. Isabella was killing me from the inside out. The woman was poison that consumed my every thought. I found my mind leaving business and wondering what she was doing instead.

What alliance was she forging... What new charity was she supporting... What else was up her sleeve...

Isabella Agostino was intelligent, beautiful, successful. She was *my* wife. Yet I was fucking some whore who mopped the bathroom in my bar and made mediocre cocktails.

Fuck. I was such an asshole.

"Mario, are you listening?" Fina waved a hand in my face. "Mario!"

"Fuck! What, Fina! Jesus-fucking-Christ. I told you not to come here." I swiped my papers off the desk, stormed to my feet, and leaned in her face. "I have enough shit on my plate without—"

"He's picked a husband for me! Some old man from Sicily!" Her eyes welled up with tears before she collapsed into my arms.

"Don't worry. Your father is aware of my decision on who you should marry. And my word is law," I grunted.

"You won't leave your wife. You won't even speak to me. But somehow, *now,* you have the power to pick a husband for me?" Fina's anger was her downfall.

"Watch. Your. Tone," I warned.

"You son of a bitch! I came here to make you see what you're doing to me! To get you to understand that you're the only man I want." She raised a hand to slap me, and I let her. "How can you be so cruel?"

When she pulled back to swing again, I caught her wrist. "One. That's all you get." I squeezed hard, then shoved her back. "I'll find you someone better suited to benefit New York. Not Sicily."

"Now my wedding is for *your* benefit?"

"Was mine not for the same thing? We're all tied to *il famiglia*. It's our duty."

This was the part of Serafina that pissed me off the most. When she lost her temper, she'd become hyperfocused on herself. A selfish bitch. My father's voice echoed in my head.

"She's uncontrollable and a loose cannon, son."

"An alliance with the west will make you a queen," I said, and watched her eyes round out while a glint of greed burned bright. "Sal Ragetti Junior is preparing to take over Cali. Your engagement to him will ensure peace on both coasts."

The Ragettis had twice the numbers we did. Even with everything Isabella was doing to increase our reach, it wouldn't be enough to match theirs. The patriarch—Sal Senior—had been making strategic alliances for the last two decades. New York *needed* this leg up. Lucky for us, Senior wanted peace as much as I did. And it seemed his son had taken a liking to Fina.

"I won't do it." She stood tall. Defiant.

"You will. Besides, it's already done. And before you utter another fucking word, Fina, remember who the fuck you're talking to. I already told you the days of *us* are over." She flinched when I crowded her space and dropped my voice. "You know, Mark already told me how you cornered my wife in the bathroom. What did you say to her?"

"I… Nothing." She shrugged before appearing to think better of it. "What did she tell you?"

I laughed and licked at my lips. "Isabella wouldn't waste her breath mentioning you."

Fina and I glared at each other, neither of us speaking for several long minutes. I could see her hatred for me and I didn't care. Maybe it was because I knew all along that Serafina was never capable of being the wife I needed. What I needed was at home waiting for me. Pregnant with my child while I was drowning myself in booze and pussy.

"When?" Fina asked.

"I'm arranging to have Sal fly to New York in a few weeks."

"I hate you," she whispered before spinning on her heels and walking back out the door.

Turning to my whiskey, I tossed it back and quickly refilled it. When the burn didn't seem to help, I threw the empty glass against the wall. The broken pieces did little to stifle my rage and I began trashing my office.

"Sir?" Mags stuck her head in the room, her eyes bouncing around at the destruction. "Want me to come back?" She raised a broom and dustpan.

"No. Get it done." I sat back behind my desk and watched her.

The whiskey was altering my brain as images of Isabella danced in front of my eyes. Her smile and laughter made my heart lighter. Laying my head back against the chair, I chuckled to myself as I thought about her anger. My dick got hard at the way she held her own against me.

Where Fina's anger made her rash, Isabella's highlighted her confidence. She didn't need to raise her voice or a hand to get her point across. My wife was elegant in everything she did. Even when it came to unleashing her anger.

A hand went to my belt and I didn't stop it. I kept my eyes closed, trying to breathe through my mouth to avoid the stench of Mags's perfume. Her lips wrapped around my cock. I grabbed onto her hair, taking control as I fucked her throat like I fucked her pussy. She retched and scratched against me, but I didn't care. I was enjoying the feel of my balls against her chin. Until her teeth scraped against my dick, and I threw her off me.

I pulled her to her feet and motioned towards the condom. "Put it on me and bend over the desk." I stumbled and couldn't see right.

Mags's ass was in the air. Her pussy glistened. And without warning, I shoved deep inside her. The desk skidded across the floor as I fucked all my rage into her. She screamed and begged for more, her fake moans nothing like the sweet mewls my wife offered me.

"Mario!" Rick pounded on the wall. I pounded harder into Mags's cunt, my release within my grasp. Serafina was behind him, smirking as she watched me cheat on my wife.

"Get. Out. Almost. Done," I grunted, my balls pulled tight, and I spilled into the condom.

"Isabella is on her way to the hospital. Something's wrong with the baby."

I stumbled, my dick swinging free as my heart beat out of my chest for an entirely different reason now.

"You good?" Rick watched my face, probably wondering if I cared enough to go.

I reached a hand down to remove the condom, but it was already gone. So I tucked my dick back into my pants and stormed down the hall with Rick hot on my heels. We'd just made it to the main barroom when he caught up to me.

"What happened?" I hissed.

"She's bleeding. That's all I know." He shrugged.

"Boss! We got a problem." One of my men raised the phone from behind the bar. "Mrs. Agostino and Mark are stuck in the elevator at the penthouse. Seems to be a power outage of some sort."

"Let's go!" I tugged Rick forward and we charged outside, jumping into the car and making it back to the penthouse in record time.

We'd just arrived and stepped into the lobby when the power came back on and the elevator doors were opening. My heart seized in my chest the moment I saw her. Isabella resting on Mark's chest, his arms around her. My fists clenched at my sides until I noticed all the blood. Around her and on his shirt.

"My car is out front." I snatched Isabella from his arms and ran.

"That perfume doesn't suit you, by the way."

Her harsh tone had me stumbling as I approached the car door. Deciding it was best not to argue at the moment, I set her inside without another word. Isabella was pale while the red seeping through her clothes was a stark contrast. She'd been through hell while I was balls-deep in another woman. If that wasn't enough to send me straight to hell, nothing else could.

The doctors rushed Isabella inside as soon as we arrived at the hospital, and I was told to stay in the waiting room. My men, Rick, Frances, and Mark all showed up a short time later. We sat in tension-riddled silence as the fear of the unknown seemed to thicken the air around us.

"Mr. Agostino?" a man in a lab coat called out, and I darted forward. "Your wife and baby are okay. They're both very lucky. This happens to about one out of four women, while more than half of those instances result in miscarriages."

"But they're… okay?" Frances whimpered.

"Yes. Sir, if you'd follow me, I will take you to your wife now." The doctor opened a door and waved me inside.

I stared down at her, so pale and motionless while the size of the bed made her seem even smaller. I pulled up a chair and continued to watch her for the next few hours.

Why did I do this shit to her? If I'd just gotten her the damn house… If I'd just stayed home and told her how I felt… So many *ifs* in this equation. But in the end, none of them mattered when this was my reality.

"I lost the baby, didn't I?" Isabella's soft voice snapped me back to the present.

"No. The baby is okay," I said as her eyes filled with tears. "Bella, I'm so—" My words died off, and I glanced towards the door as a doctor and nurse walked in.

"How are Mom and Dad doing?" They moved around the hospital bed, forcing me to stand back, as they pulled up an ultrasound machine. I could hear my heart beating in my ears even as they assured me this was all routine.

Isabella had been going to her appointments and Mark had been filling me in afterwards. But I'd been too much of a coward to escort her myself, choosing to blame my work. Truth was I could've made the time, should've made the time. But I hadn't.

"Would you like to know the gender of the baby?" the nurse asked.

Isabella glanced at me with hope in her eyes. I smiled, wrapping my arms around her shoulders, and nodded. Then the nurse moved the device across Isabella's stomach, and together we watched the screen.

"Congratulations. It appears you're having a boy."

The medical team gave us a few more updates before leaving the room again.

"A boy." Isabella grinned. "Your heir."

That one word was like a punch to the gut. It was true that every *capo* needed an heir. It was what was expected, and we'd done it on our first try.

Would she cut me out now?

"We should call him Lucky." She chuckled. "They said he was very lucky to survive—that it was a miracle."

"He's lucky he didn't hurt you," I grunted in reply, and I could feel her glare penetrate me.

Yes, I wanted a son, a family with this woman. Needed one. But the thought of losing her settled heavy in my gut.

I slid onto the hospital bed, and Isabella rested her head against my chest. For a singular moment, she just let me hold on to her. Our silent embrace spoke louder than any argument. We had shit we needed to work out between us.

Going rigid as she inhaled a deep breath, Isabella pulled away from me, muttering, "You should head home." She rolled onto her side, giving me her back.

I never showered while I waited for her to wake up. I considered yelling at her. For allowing me to feel something towards her. For becoming a complication that I didn't want or need.

"Boss. You've got a call." Mark leaned into the room, smiling at my wife before quickly locking it down. "West coast."

"Find the doctor. I want her home." I waited for his nod of understanding before turning to face Isabella again. "I'll be back to pick you up."

"Mark can take me."

"I said I will do it." I leaned in to kiss her, but her death glare gave me pause. "I will. Me. Not him," I clarified, then pivoted on my heel while calling out to Mark to follow me. "I need to get this shit with Sal handled. I don't want any of this to touch her." I stopped in front of the elevator. "Don't enter that fucking room. You stand outside the door until I return. Got it?"

I knew it was petty, but it made me feel better.

The moment I entered the penthouse, I made a beeline for the shower, changed into clean clothes, and started plotting. I'd already arranged to have Sal spend a weekend in New York. We'd discuss business, then he'd meet Fina. I made a quick call to update her on the when and where, and she hung up without a word.

"Good evening, Mr. Agostino."

I looked up from my desk as the fake blonde with fake tits and a fake smile was escorted into my office. My realtor. I'd fucked her a few times in the past before I settled on buying this penthouse. Now, as she greedily took me in, I had no idea what I'd seen in her before.

"My *wife* is expecting our first son and we need a new home." I didn't miss the irritation flick across her face as I passed her the piece of paper I had laid out in front of me. "Those are my expectations, and once you narrow down a list, my wife will tell you which one she prefers."

"Okay."

"And if I get word—at all—that you mention anything about your loose pussy bouncing on my cock..." I pushed to my feet, stepped around the desk, and backed the woman into the closest wall. "I'll give your hefty commission to someone else and pass your cheap ass around to my men."

She cleared her throat. "When will Mrs. Agostino be available?"

CHAPTER 11
SERAFINA

His pompous attitude used to be so attractive. Not anymore. His behavior as *capo* was pushing me over the edge. Mario was the love of my life. A love that I thought was special. Uncommon. However, if a man truly loved you, would he be so quick to jump in someone else's bed?

He could lie and tell me his new wife meant something to him. But I wasn't an idiot. He was the same old Mario. He'd stray, seek comfort elsewhere, but he always came back to me. Now he was throwing it all away for a woman who meant nothing to him. Watching him fuck Mags told me everything I needed to know. While it seemed the hooks Isabella had sunk into him were deep and steadfast—I had no doubt the bitch warned him off me—made men were still made men.

And they were all cheaters.

As I watched their car pull away, my temper flickered and my thoughts calmed. If this was really what he wanted, to toss me aside, I'd ruin him. The promise of California did hold a certain excitement. I'd always known I would be the perfect *capo's* wife.

California had an even greater reach than New York. But this city was my home and Mario was supposed to rule it with *me*.

"Fucking asshole." Mags wandered back into the bar, straightening her clothes and muttering under her breath.

"Trouble in paradise?" I smirked at her scowl. "Get me a dirty martini."

Women like Mags knew where they belonged. I watched her mouth drop, likely some smart-ass remark on her tongue until she thought better of it and turned towards the liquor bottles.

That's right. At least *someone* knew better than to fuck with me.

She slid the glass across the bar top, the olives bouncing around the bottom, and as I took a sip, my anger hit its crescendo.

Fuck him.

Mario was supposed to handle his wife. Get rid of her. Toss her ass off a bridge. Be the *capo* of the goddamn mafia and fucking end her. Then I'd take my rightful place at his side. He was not supposed to order me across the country. If he were a real man—a real *capo*—then he would take out the Ragettis and ensure the east dominated the west.

Two more martinis and my decision was made. If Mario didn't want to see the error of his ways, I'd have to show him myself. There was one man I knew who hated Mario more than I did. One man who was dumb enough to help me and weak enough for me to control.

"That looks like the face of a woman with a plan." Rick dropped onto the stool to my right. "Penny for your thoughts?"

"Shouldn't you be at the hospital praying for your boss's *bastard?*"

Rick watched as I suggestively sucked on my olive before finally biting down.

"The baby is fine." His tongue traced his lips as he watched me pluck the second one from my glass.

"Of course it is," I huffed before tossing back what was left of my martini. "Don't you get tired of it, Rick? That man owning you, *il famiglia,* and running it right into the fucking ground."

"You're drunk, Fina." The metal legs of his stool squeaked on the wood flooring as he dragged it closer. "Get her another and me a Scotch."

Mags's eyes flicked back and forth between us, her brows reaching her hairline. Rick tucked a loose tendril behind my ear, his finger trailing down my neck to my shoulder. A quick swoop across my breasts made my nipples harden.

"Now," he barked, and Mags jumped at his order, throwing worried glances my way as she poured the drinks.

"Fuck. Off." I flicked a hand out and shooed her aside.

"Bitch." She tossed her hair over her shoulder and disappeared into the back room.

"Care to share what's running through that pretty little head of yours?"

"Me? I'm just a woman." I batted my lashes and lifted a hand to my chest with feigned innocence.

"A woman with a brain."

"How. Dangerous," I taunted. "If you must know, Rick, I'm tired. Tired of not getting what *I* want." Abandoning my drink, I pivoted in my seat to face him. My bare legs fit between his, my toes rubbing down his shins. A seductive woman was also a powerful one. Something that became all too clear as I watched his eyes blaze, his breath bated as he waited to see what I would do next. "What do you want, Rick?"

His mouth opened as I dropped an olive inside.

"Tell me." I licked a drop of vodka off his chin before meeting his eye again. "What do you want?"

"Don't fuck with me, Fina." His control was slipping as his guard dropped along with it.

Then I saw exactly what I needed. A man whose best friend was handed everything he had wanted for himself. Including me.

Glass shattered as Rick's hand swept across the bar before he lifted me out of my seat and dropped me face-first onto the solid veneer. My arms stretched out to grip the edge as he tore my shirt open, kicked my legs apart, and inhaled.

"Fuck, you smell amazing." He buried his nose between my thighs before his tongue lapped at my center.

"Fuck me, Rick." All I heard was the click of a belt and the rustle of clothes, and then he was buried deep inside me. "Yes!"

The vodka warmed my gut and slowed my brain as the feel of him calmed my anger. Until I glanced over and saw Mags staring at me with a smirk playing on her lips.

Fuck. You.

Rick's grunts peppered the air as he fucked me from behind while my mind ran a mile a minute.

Could I get him on my side? Get him to kill his best friend and take over?

"You fucking bitch." He slapped my ass hard enough to sober me up again. "Now I'm good enough to fuck? Because you're pissed at him?"

The pain in my abdomen and the fire lighting up my skin were taking over as my orgasm ebbed farther and farther away.

"Fuck." His breaths came out faster, his thrusts disjointed as he hissed next to my ear. "Stupid bitch. He'll never want you." Rick pulled out and grabbed my hair, tugging me off the bar. The look he gave me was one of pure loathing as he twisted my locks in his grip and forced me onto my knees. "Dumb cunt. Stay there, on the floor, where you fucking belong until I leave."

Hacking back a gob of his spit, he pulled it around his mouth a few times before lodging it in my direction. Then the bastard stomped away as I grabbed onto the bar and pushed myself to my knees. My body felt bruised and battered but all I could do was watch him as he straightened his belt, opened the door, and turned back to look at me.

"You think you're fucking special, but you've always been just a hole to him. To any man. Look at you now. You're exactly where you belong." He laughed before stepping through the door. "A dirty cunt with my seed leaking out of her."

Without thinking, I flipped him off. Which had him slamming the door closed again and charging forward. He ripped me from my spot and shoved me onto my stomach. Spreading my legs and plunging his fingers inside me. Twisting and turning until I cried out at the pain.

"Open your fucking mouth." His grip on my jaw left me no choice but to comply. "Taste me, bitch. Suck me fucking clean." He shoved his fingers inside my mouth until I was sputtering for air.

He pulled them back out again and I swiped a hand over my face to wipe away the spittle. "Fuck you. You piece of shit."

His body tensed and he dropped his weight on my back. "No. Fuck you."

I heard his zipper before he started roughly fucking me again. One hand pressed down on my lower back, the other on the side of my head. He pushed on my face, the pain shooting through my jaw and rattling my teeth. Everything hurt as the skin on my cheek and stomach took the brunt of Rick's weight. Until, thankfully, he finally came again.

He laughed, shoving off me and walking out the door without another word.

Several minutes passed as I attempted to calm my racing heart and order my body to move. But between his brutal assault and my broken pride, I was frozen to the spot. Even as I heard footsteps approach and men chuckle just beyond the door.

"Come on. They'll just take more from you." Mags sighed while she tugged me to my feet and rushed me into the back room.

"Don't fucking touch me." I shrugged out of her hold.

"Wow. Cum spilling down your leg and you still think you're better than me." Her laugh mocked me. "Hurts… doesn't it? Being just another dumb whore for the rest of 'em to use." She slung her purse strap over one shoulder and pivoted on her heel before pausing at the door to glance at me. Or rather past me. Her fingers raked down her arms while the dazed look in her eye caught me off guard.

Was she fucking high?

"All of you think you're somethin' because your last names end in vowels. You fucked up underestimating me." The outside light was blinding as the door creaked open and she stepped out.

"Where the fuck are you going, Mags?" The bitch had a death wish if she thought she could come for *il famiglia.*

"Philly." She smirked.

"He'll kill you. If Metro doesn't, Mario will." I told her what we both knew. She didn't answer as the door clicked closed. "Whelp, I guess you're a dumb, *dead* whore now." She left me alone with my thoughts, which was dangerous for everyone.

If Rick wasn't going to help me get what I wanted, I'd have to find someone who would. It was time I made my move.

CHAPTER 12

SERAFINA

Several weeks later, I wandered through the junkyard, ignoring the catcalls as my hips swayed. My heels sank into the mud as I locked my Mercedes and wandered towards the warehouse. The guard outside watched me curiously before his arm shot out to stop me from entering. His eyes hungrily took in my short, hip-hugging skirt. And a moment later, he opened the door and I felt his glare on my ass as I brushed past him.

Cars were parked along each wall as laughter and voices drifted from the back. The office door was wide open and I stalked inside with my head held high. Several men loomed around the room, cigarettes in their hands and smirks playing on their lips. The sudden silence sent a shiver down my spine.

"Well, well, well. If it isn't Mario's little pet."

Anthony Moretti was a decent-looking man. A bit on the shorter side but not a total waste. Where Mario was all muscle, Anthony was a little pudgy around his midsection. He pulled on his cigarette, leaning forward and blowing the smoke in my face.

"Why do I get the feeling you're about to cry on my shoulder and tell me all of Mario's secrets?"

The room erupted with laughter. I ignored the obnoxious sound.

"Fine. Guess you don't want to know." I went to pivot on my heel, but his hand moved at lightning speed to snatch my wrist.

"Everyone out," he barked, and the rest of them made themselves scarce while muttering crude comments under their breath. "Speak."

"Mario doesn't realize this city deserves better. He picked that Sicilian trash—that nobody—over me."

Anthony took a step closer. "Isabella Bruno is quite entrancing. She has half of New York's elite eating out of her hand. What would you bring to the table, Serafina?"

My dress was tight, revealing, as his eyes licked over every inch of my exposed skin. Anthony was… complicated. He seemed intelligent enough but was always one step behind Mario. A nuisance more than a challenge. But, with my help, that could change.

I needed this to work. My clock was ticking. And fast.

My hand dropped to my stomach. Not only had Rick bruised my body and my ego in equal measure, but he'd also left me with a parting gift. My plan was to help Anthony ruin Mario, wrap him around my finger, and then disappear before I started to show. Once my son was born, I'd give him up for adoption.

I couldn't tell you how, but I just knew I was carrying the boy Mario should have given me.

I gasped, thrown back into the present as Anthony lifted me onto his desk before stepping between my thighs. My breasts were ready to spill out of the dress and he traced the lace edges. Without asking for my permission, he wrapped his lips around mine and filled my mouth with his smokey tongue.

"I should fuck you, mark you, and then dump you on that prick's doorstep."

"Why would you when I can help you beat him?" I grabbed onto Anthony's tie and quickly tugged him forward. "Rule New York together."

"Rule? Together?" He laughed in my face. "I want a warm cunt to birth my sons." His hands ran up my thighs and I had to clench my teeth to stop the tears from falling.

I'd show them all I was worth more than this.

I stumbled against Anthony's chest as he pulled me from the desk and ripped my dress over my head. I stood tall in my matching lingerie as his lips curled into a pleased smirk. And I couldn't help but hate myself as I felt my panties get wet beneath the touch of his calloused fingers.

"Is that you, Fina? Will you take my cum and give me kids, then fuck off until I call you back to my bed? Because your pussy feels warm and tight, and honestly that's all I really need." He pressed his fingers inside me. "Turn around and bend over the desk. I want a taste of what you have to offer."

Anthony spun me around again. I cried out in shock as he tugged my panties up so they pulled tight and shredded against my skin. Then he kicked my legs farther apart and shoved my face against the desk's veneer.

This wasn't the part where I expected anyone to feel sorry for me. It was the world I was born into. Women were nothing more than wet holes to the men surrounding us. Which was exactly why we needed to climb that ladder. Be at the top where only a select few could touch us.

"Fuck!" I screamed when Anthony slammed into me. It wasn't because of his size either. It was because of the way my knees smacked against the wooden surface, how his hands clawed at and pinched my skin, his thrusts punishing and not pleasure-inducing. My arms shook as they struggled to bear our combined weight, and I stared at the papers under us as my tears dripped down my cheeks.

Anthony pulled free, turned me around to face him, and set my ass on his desk. He gripped my neck and my legs wrapped around him. I swallowed, scratching at his hands when he tightened his hold. His lips traced mine softly before biting down. He was brutal, vicious, laughing as I felt my consciousness slip through his fingertips.

Until he finally let go.

Anthony stared at where our bodies met between my thighs, fluid leaking out onto the papers beneath me, and grinned at the implication. While everything inside me wanted to tell him that it didn't matter. Because someone else had already knocked me up.

"Get the fuck out. I'll call you when I want my dick wet again." He waved a dismissive hand before shoving himself back into his pants with a grunt. "That was decent, Fina. But now I see why Mario didn't fight all that hard to keep you."

"Fuck you." I grabbed my purse and turned to leave.

My hand had just reached the door when Anthony slammed it closed again. His expression softened as he smiled and stroked my face. "Come on, baby. Tell me all his secrets." He guided me over to the leather sofa next to his desk and sat me down.

After several moments of indecision, I finally caved. This was my chance to show Mario he chose the wrong woman. To marry *and* to fuck over. The meeting with the west was Anthony's chance to take the reins. My father would agree to any alliance that ended in his favor.

"Mario's in discussions with the west. He wants me to marry Sal Ragetti."

"If Mario and Sal align their interests, they'll have a monopoly that spans both coasts." Anthony's jaw clenched tight as he stomped to his desk and swiped up the phone. "I'm not the only one who sees a problem with that."

"Sal is already on his way," I warned, and Anthony just smirked at me.

"Hey, JP." He spoke into the phone. "It's been a long time, old friend. Remember all those conversations about succession?" Anthony paused to listen before replying, "Your brother is headed to New York to solidify an alliance with the Agostinos."

JP?

John Paul Ragetti. Sal's brother. Rumor had it the guy was a fucking lunatic on a tight leash. Of course, he'd be friends with Anthony. Commiserating over the shitty positions' life had landed them in.

"I will hold up my end if you hold up yours." Anthony grinned into the phone before hanging up and stalking back in my direction. "Serafina, you just got what you wanted. That marriage is as dead as your future husband and soon you'll be all mine." He kissed me roughly, tapped my ass, and shoved me towards the door.

My head held high, I quickly made my way back to the junkyard. My resolve was waning as I threw the car into reverse and pulled out of the lot. I pushed the pedal done and hauled ass as I watched the warehouse disappear in my rearview.

What the hell had I done?

I was as good as dead if Mario found out. Worse if Anthony failed to deliver. My anger had gotten the best of me and now I was royally fucked.

"They're going to kill me." I paced the bathroom at Isabella's gala.

Shit had been insane these last few weeks. Sal came… and died. JP threatened to start a war, but his father handled it. I didn't know what Mario did to keep the peace, but they seemed to just accept the story of a robbery gone wrong. Anthony and JP's plot had been twisted and Mario continued to control the narrative.

My stomach was growing, and any day now, people would know. I needed to go into hiding. And soon. Rumor had it that Mario knew Anthony was involved in the murder. And now Anthony was looking for me to hold up my end of the deal. Which meant that Mario would put two and two together in no time.

"Are you all right?"

I jumped, glancing up into the mirror to see Isabella staring back at me. She was poised and elegant while her dress pulled tight around her baby bump. She was everything you'd expect of the *capo's* wife.

I'd wanted to ruin this woman. Take everything from her. But now I was ready to grovel. Reduced to waiting in a bathroom with tears running down my face and my hand resting protectively over my unborn child.

I slid down the wall until my rear hit the floor. "I… I fucked up so bad. I know I don't deserve your help." I dropped my head into my hands and sucked in a breath. "I just loved him so much. I wanted everything you have and now I've fucked it all up."

Isabella glanced down at the hand still clutching my belly. "Is it Mario's?"

I shook my head. "Rick's." Her eyes rounded, and I was quick to clarify. "He doesn't know. I want to run. I want to have this baby… before I give him away."

"You sure about that?" she asked, and I nodded.

"Rick will never claim him as his own, and the boy will be called a bastard. My family… if they knew… my father would kill me for shaming him."

"Anthony Moretti is telling everyone you're engaged, you know."

I peered up to meet her eye. Isabella was truly beautiful inside and out. It was a shame, the way women were raised to hate each other. Pitted against one another since birth. Comparing status, beauty, intelligence. I hated this woman because she had what I wanted. What I thought I deserved more than her.

"I was horrible to you. I'm sorry. I know I don't deserve your kindness… I just don't…" I shook my head, unable to continue.

"We all make decisions when our hands are forced." She spoke thoughtfully. I caught her expression, but she wasn't looking at me. "And then we deal. Now come." She reached out a hand and helped me off the floor.

A moment passed between us as I confessed everything I'd done. Sal's death, Anthony and JP's involvement, all of it. She paused when I was done before calling Mark into the bathroom. He scowled in my direction but returned his attention to Isabella when she addressed him. They were going to get me out of the city. Out of the country. She would call in favors and use every connection at her disposal to help me hide out in Sicily.

"He's not going to like this," Mark muttered under his breath as we pulled away from the venue.

"Good thing he's too busy with the senator to notice my absence, now isn't it?" Isabella ran a hand over her swollen belly as her face contorted with pain. She breathed through it before turning her glare on me. "Anthony isn't going to stop, Fina."

"I know," I whispered.

"When you return, you will come to me. You will do what you need to do for your child. And then I'll cash in on this favor."

Her tone sparked a latent fury inside me, but I had to force it aside. If she turned her back on me, I'd end up dead. There was no way out of this. I'd made my bed, and now I had to curl up at Isabella's feet and lie on it.

"The only way any of this works, Fina, is if you marry Anthony. Giving our newfound friendship the nourishment it needs to blossom. I want to know everything that man does. Every move he makes. And then your debt to me will be paid."

I could see the way Mark was looking at her. He was as surprised as I was.

"If not, I will tell Rick, Mario, and the Ragettis…" She nodded at my belly. "…*everything.*"

This was not how things were supposed to be. Anthony was supposed to rule New York by now, an alliance forged with JP thanks to me. Instead, bodies were piling up and I was tipping over into my own grave. None of these men would protect me after they learned all the different parts I'd played.

We pulled down a long driveway and headed to a small private airport just outside the city. I'd gotten myself into this mess, and Isabella was getting me out of it. It tasted bitter on my tongue to admit defeat.

I reached out an arm, gripping the door while intending to slide out. But her sharp grasp on my elbow stopped me short. "I mean it. My men will have eyes on you in Sicily. I expect you back at first chance." As if to emphasize her point, a few guys in suits stood shoulder-to-shoulder in front of the car. "They're loyal to my father and to me. They will protect you and the baby. Until you give birth. Then you will marry him. Become my eyes and ears in that house."

"I know. I owe you my life."

"This is a little secret between us girls. Because if it ever gets out that you were involved, you'll have an even larger target on your back."

"And Anthony?"

Isabella scoffed. "He's a man. He won't tell anyone that a *woman* was involved in his failed attempt to overthrow my husband. And besides, he needs Mario's help to keep the peace. But to maintain it, I need you back here."

I nodded before closing the door and turning towards *her* loyal men. I should've had an entourage of people at my beck and call. I should've had, done, been so much more. Mario had always warned me that my anger would destroy me. And I loathed that he was right. I allowed more men to hurt me. I allowed men to continue to take from me. And in turn, I was now indebted to the most powerful woman in New York. The same woman *I* wanted to be.

But as the plane took off, and I watched the city slowly disappear below me, I made myself a promise. I'd return stronger than ever. New York and I weren't done. I'd get my happily ever after.

Somehow.

CHAPTER 13

CHAPTER 13
MARIO

"**W**here the fuck were you?" I stormed into the bedroom, the door slamming against the wall with an audible thud.

"Excuse me?" Isabella placed her book on the end table, dropped her hands into her lap, and peered up at me with indifference.

I was in a private meeting with the senator when I was informed that my wife had left early. Without my knowledge and without the decency of telling me where she was going. "What the fuck happened?"

"Mario, seriously? You were chatting and I was tired." She shrugged.

Tired. She was tired.

The devil himself couldn't keep up with the shit that had been happening over these last few months. I thought Isabella and I had settled into a routine. I left the house to tend to the various businesses during the day, but I'd been home every night.

The new house was three stories tall with an understated lavishness that only my wife could pull off. She'd been decorating the nursery and I'd been attending all her doctors' visits. Our son was strong and healthy as we counted down the days until he finally made his entrance into the world.

Like I said, I *believed* things had fallen into place. My home life, my recent political connections, my position as *capo*. However, every time it appeared as though I had one thing under control, something else fell apart.

Instead of arguing with the woman, I climbed into bed with her. Our bodies did the talking and I chased the relief she brought me. It was clear our relationship had shifted, but it still wasn't what either of us desired. At the same time, I was too busy and too much of a prick to do anything about it.

Discussions between Rick and me were strained as well. He'd been missing important meetings and reneging on his obligations. Add in the shit with the west, and I didn't have time to babysit grown men. Sal Junior dying in my city was a clusterfuck. His father was trying to keep the peace and I was paying out the ass for it. He and I had a silent agreement to sweep the incident under the rug. For a price, of course. While the guilty party was more than willing to empty his pockets to pay for my silence.

That said, the younger Ragetti brother was still causing a bit of a stir. Sal's death meant JP was next in line to replace his father. He wanted blood—to situate himself atop the organization. Problem was, he was going about it the wrong way and garnering a lot of unwanted attention. As well as some loyal followers. And anyone who knew anything about this life also knew crazy attracted crazy.

My biggest issue was the fact that Sal wanted a corpse. A body for a body. A complication I was keeping to myself. At least until it suited me. You see, the Morettis had one thing I'd wanted. Access to the docks off the Hudson. Anthony's father owned a huge import-export business and I wanted the profits.

And I fucking owned Anthony now.

A rash, power-hungry man was also a foolish one. He had no

recourse, no protection from the fallout. The Ragettis wanted blood and JP would kill Anthony. Which meant I was the only thing standing between Anthony and the end of a hot barrel. If he didn't learn to heel, I'd deliver his ass to Cali myself. Anthony couldn't so much as take a piss without asking for *my* permission first. I was keeping him on a tight leash because I knew it was only a matter of time before he'd start plotting behind my back again.

And then there was Fina. My plans to tie her to the west died with Sal, seeing as JP already had a bride. So Fina was newly engaged to Anthony Moretti. Their union would allow me to control them both, increasing my hold on the docks in exchange for keeping Anthony's secret.

I hadn't bothered to check in with her, learning she'd disappeared around the same time as Mags. Rick had been working on tracking them down, to ensure that they weren't interfering in anything. And his piss poor attitude was grating on my very limited patience. I'd been so goddamn busy I didn't have time to breathe, let alone cater to his bullshit.

Rick lowered himself onto the bar stool next to mine, ordering the new girl to grab him a Scotch. "What crawled up your ass now?"

"Watch your fucking tone, Rick." I swiped up my glass and downed half the contents. "I'm still your fucking *capo* and I deserve respect."

I was on edge and nothing seemed to help. The new girl had just finished sucking my dick, but I was hard again thinking of my wife. Home. Alone. Add the stress of this entire organization, and my sanity was waning.

"Why would Serafina be hiding in Sicily?" he said, suddenly garnering my attention. "Michele's property."

"The fuck are you talking about? The man's been in the States since learning he'd be a grandfather."

"Then why are there guards at his compound and whispers

about the woman he's keeping there?" Rick shrugged. "I mean, it's not like the old fuck has to hide a mistress. His wife's been dead and buried for ages now. Strange how Isabella never mentioned them having company…"

I grunted in response, but the truth was that wasn't the only odd thing about my wife's behavior of late. Something seemed off. I just couldn't put my finger on it.

Then a recent conversation came to mind.

Several months ago, Rick and I had been discussing Fina's disappearance when Isabella entered the room and began fussing with one of her vases. At the time, I didn't give it a second thought.

"*I*t's probably for the best. Needs time before her pending nuptials.*"

"Yeah." I was barely paying attention as my eyes tracked Isabella's every movement. She pivoted on her heel and flitted back towards the door. "Wait… I need you to plan the wedding. I'll have several high-profile families in attendance, and I can't have Fina using this as her opportunity to make a scene. I need this to be a tasteful affair."

"Of course. Whatever you need, husband. I'll get started now." Isabella nodded before slowly clicking the door closed behind her.

*O*nly now did I realize she never asked me *when*. In fact, the entire event had been planned without requiring any input.

"I need to go…" I ground out as I stumbled towards the door.

"Where you going?" Rick called after me.

To fuck the lies out of my wife. I kept that last part to myself.

~

"You're home early," Isabella hummed as she closed the book she was reading.

"Keeping tabs, are you?"

She rolled her eyes while struggling to get to her feet. That's what happened. I entered a room, she left. I'd tried breaking down her walls. Tried to be better to her. And for her. Instead, I kept fucking up. Now… was no different.

"Where is she?" I hissed, watching her face for a reaction. She refused to give me one. "Where, Isabella?"

"Who, Mario?" The coldness in her voice was new, however. "Missing your whore, are you?"

"What. Did. You. Do." Chest heaving, I stormed across the room.

"What did I do?" she challenged me. "Me? What did *I* do?" The storm clouds were looming and it wouldn't be long before all hell broke loose.

"Why was Serafina spotted at your father's property?" I'd expected surprise, maybe even a little shame, not the devious smirk currently playing on her lips.

"What. Did. I. Do." She poked my chest with each word. "Since my freedom was stolen, I've done nothing but put you first. The *famiglia* first. Galas, committees, benefits, stupid-as-fuck luncheons. All of it. Every day. Working my ass off to take *you* to the next level. You're fucking untouchable now, Mario."

This fire. This version of my wife was my favorite.

"And instead of thanking me… instead of giving me *anything,* you come here demanding to know what I've done with your whore?" Now she was shouting. "How about you ask me what she did and why I helped her?"

"The fuck are you talking about?"

Her lips curled into a snarl. "How do you think Anthony Moretti knew where Sal would be?"

No, Fina wouldn't have done that.

"Because your little whore has a terrible temper and fucking told him."

"She wouldn't do that," I repeated aloud this time.

Isabella laughed in my face. "Poor Mario. The woman he loves made a fool of him." She leveled her glare at me. "Well. Fuck. You. This is the last time I clean up one of your messes."

Tears filled her eyes and I hated that my instinct was to hold her. I ignored it. Too consumed by my anger at Fina. At my wife. At it all.

"Don't worry. She'll be back in a few months to attend the beautiful wedding I've planned for her. And then your little whore will be *my* plaything."

"What does that mean?"

Isabella paused in the doorway. "It means… *that* betrayal wasn't her first. But when she comes back, she'll be my eyes and ears in the Moretti compound… for you. You're welcome, husband. Your reach is infinite."

Time stood still long after Isabella was gone. Once more, I'd underestimated the woman. Even worse, I'd underestimated Fina's stupidity. Whatever the fuck she did, my wife owned her now. A realization that made me murderous. For a different reason altogether. I hated being purposefully left in the dark.

"Mark!" I barked out before turning on my heel and stomping into my office. I could hear his footsteps trailing behind me. "My *wife* isn't to leave this house until she's in fucking labor."

The look of shock and indecision on his face was just further proof that my men's allegiance was to my wife. And it made me furious.

"Is there a fucking problem?" I grunted, cutting him off before he could respond. "The doctors can make home visits. The senator's wife can visit too. But no one else. Like I said, Isabella is not to leave. Now get the fuck out of my face."

My phone began ringing as the door closed behind him. "You've got a problem, *mi amico*," Metro hummed into the phone. "I've got a little bird that flew all the way to Philly. And she's ready to tell me all your secrets for a price."

Fina? No fucking way…

"The name Mags ring a bell?"

I started cursing under my breath.

"Well, she's here. Started slinging drinks at one of my local spots. Tried to get a meeting, name dropping, and all that jazz…"

"Christ. I don't fucking need this right now." I ran a tired hand down my face. "She said anything?"

"Little tidbits here and there. Nothing of any real significance. She's waiting on me." He talked to someone in the background. "She's on her way up now. Want me to put you on speaker?"

No, no, I didn't.

"Yes," I said anyway.

A door opened, then closed before the click of heels followed it. "Rumor has it you have some news for me." I could hear Metro's grin all the way down the line.

"My, I can't believe such a strong, powerful man like you hasn't taken over New York yet."

"Power has nothing to do with it, honey." Metro moved closer to the phone. "Why're you in my city?"

"I've heard about you. Heard you're a man who can help someone disappear… for a price."

"And what makes you think I'd help you? Tell me what you have to offer me and I'll consider it."

And just like that, the bitch I'd taken off the street. The bitch I'd helped get off drugs more times than I could count… exposed a long-serrated blade… and stabbed me in the fucking back—over and over. The stories, the details, shit I didn't even remember her being around to witness. It was circumstantial, at best, if she tried to turn any of it over to the cops. But still. A rat was a rat. And she was one dead rat.

"Did you get all that, Mario?"

"Mario?" she gasped, and I grinned.

"You're mine now, you fucking cunt," I hissed into the phone. I could hear her begging. Pleading.

"Boys!" Metro called out. Then there was shuffling, and she shrieked.

"I want to deal with her myself, but I can't leave the city right now."

"Two of my men will bring her to you with a gift for Isabella and the baby."

"Thanks, Metro. And congrats on your son. I hope your wife liked the jewelry."

"That greedy bitch? Of course she did. I'll call you once they're on their way." He cursed in Italian. "Also, you need to watch your back, my friend. JP Ragetti is telling everyone he blames you."

"Big fucking surprise."

"I'm just saying… Watch your inner circle."

These women were all sucking the life out of me. The saddest part was I'd never have expected my wife to hide something like this. I guess I gave her no choice, but it still pissed me off.

And she needed to learn that her *capo* wouldn't tolerate disobedience.

"I know. I'm huge," I huffed as Miranda helped me push up from the couch. Unsuccessfully. "Screw it. Let's eat in here."

It felt like my son would just fall out of me at any moment now. My days were long and uncomfortable, the nights even worse. Locked away in my castle. Alone. While I had no desire to go out looking and feeling like this, the lack of choice was irritating.

The bastard came and went as he pleased, but I was a prisoner. I was too far along for him to be interested in sex with me, so he returned home even later these days. That said, he did keep his promise to come to every doctor's appointment. Here. At the house. Everyone came to me.

These walls were starting to close in and I wanted out. There were times when I would catch him watching me with an odd expression on his face. Times when he'd come home drunk and curl up with a possessive arm around my stomach. If I were a stronger woman, I'd push him away. Refuse him. But in this world, I had no rights. No say in anything. And I was too damn tired to care.

"A bottle of wine? For me?" I rolled my eyes as Miranda poured herself a large glass.

"I wish you could. But since you can't, I'll drink for both of us." She smirked before sucking down a large gulp. "The boys are off somewhere, no doubt balls-deep in a couple of whores right now."

Miranda's husband loved her more than anyone I'd ever seen. And even that couldn't keep him from straying. Men in power could do what they wanted while women suffered.

"Enough about them. How is the little one? A name yet?" she asked, and I laughed because I knew she was going to hate it.

"I have one in mind." I paused before continuing. "The night I was rushed to the hospital, Mario said something that stuck with me. He'd told our son he was *lucky* he didn't kill me."

"Lucky? Isn't that a bit… Irish?" Miranda scrunched up her face like she'd eaten something sour.

"I prayed to the Devil, asked him to save my son, because I knew we were too far gone. That we live in a world God wants no part of. And I promised if he heard my prayer, I would honor him the only way I knew how." I watched Miranda's brows pinch together. "Lucifer. I'm gonna name him Lucifer. Lucky, for short."

The silence was unsettling before she finally bent over laughing, chugging her wine between chuckles. "Fuck the *capo*. His wife is terrifying. Aptly named. Love it."

I did too. My son was going to be strong. I'd raise him to be that way, to win by playing the right cards. But I'd also make sure he didn't take on his father's… *bad habits*.

Sometime later, Mark walked in to let us know that the senator was on his way. Miranda was well past drunk and ready to give him a piece of her mind. Her claws were out and her husband was going to pay.

"And Mr. Agostino?" Miranda lifted a curious brow. Mark shook his head at her question. "Motherfucker," she hissed under her breath before turning back to me. "Goodbye, darling. I'll swing by tomorrow. Don't get up." She raised a palm and stumbled out the door.

When she was out of earshot, I pinned Mark with a glare. "Where is he?"

Mark evaded the question while offering me an arm. "Would you like help?"

"That's kind of you. Don't hurt yourself."

He braced himself on the sofa and tugged me to my feet.

Climbing into bed was something else entirely, though. Mark propped the pillows behind my back and said goodnight. I didn't sleep for more than a few minutes at a time. If it wasn't the discomforts of the pregnancy, it was the nightmares that plagued me. And I would wake with a start while the memories clung to my subconsciousness.

*F*ear. *It was a new feeling—one I wasn't accustomed to. My father and his men were always around. I felt cherished, loved, and sheltered. Now, fear had me in a chokehold.*

"Hello, beautiful." The man ripped open the cupboard door and pulled me out.

He laughed as my frail teenage body thrashed against his hold. I was no match for these men, but I wouldn't cower. Even if everything inside me told me to act how I was raised—demure, appeasing. Not now. I couldn't.

"I love a good fight." He grinned as he slammed my back into the wall and pressed his body against me.

There were more of them in the room now. Laughing, watching, covered in blood.

"Don't. Touch. Me." I raised a knee, and when it connected with his balls, the other men were too shocked to grab me as I darted away, out the door, and across the lawn. The bodies of my father's

men, individuals I'd known my entire life, littered the grounds. I couldn't look at them as my bare feet stomped over the damp grass.

My attacker wasn't down for long, though. I could hear him at my back. Taunting me. "I love the chase, little girl."

His voice crawled up my spine and startled me. My foot connected with a fallen body, and I tripped and landed on the ground with a thud. The man flung himself on top of me as I struggled to get away again. He flipped me onto my back and pinned my arms above my head, his eyes filled with something dark as he pushed his bottom half against me.

Crude promises peppered my face, his breath so close I could taste it before his fist connected with my cheek. And time seemed to slow. Drag on. He lifted the hem of my dress and clawed at my panties. And as I stared into his soulless eyes, I made myself a promise.

This life was full of men just like him. They took what they wanted with no questions asked. To them, a woman was something to be used and discarded when they were done with her.

But my father had raised me to be strong. To have pride, even if I wasn't the son he needed in this world. These men wanted to take down the empire he'd built. And I wouldn't be the catalyst for my family's ruin. It was time to fight. To show everyone that a daughter could be as much of an asset as a son.

The man grunted, worn out from the chase as he tried to free himself from his pants. I might not have been able to fight him off, but I wouldn't make it easy for him either. I squirmed against his hold, and something hard poked at my side. I looked over and saw one of my father's men. Struggling to breathe and barely alive. But cognizant and loyal enough to have shimmied a knife in my direction...

~

Ahand clamped over my mouth and I struggled against it. It took me a moment to realize Mark was the culprit. He whispered for me to be quiet, a gun clutched in his free hand as he tapped his ear. And then I heard it. Something shattered in the living room before footsteps crunched over the broken pieces.

Mark helped me out of bed as the noise drew closer. "Bathroom. Lock the door."

Not again.

I moved as fast as my belly allowed me, closing myself inside the bathroom closet and crouching behind a few of the hampers, as I tried to ignore the sharp pains in my stomach.

My son was displeased, already bloodthirsty.

"Where the fuck is she?" someone shouted from the bedroom.

I closed my eyes as boots squeaked against the tile floor, followed by more clattering and crashing, as full-on chaos erupted. And I was certain Mark was fighting them off. I held my breath and prayed that he would be okay. The sounds of shuffling and grunting echoed off the bathroom walls. Then there was silence. Deafening silence.

Until someone called out from down the hall, "She's here somewhere. Keep looking!"

I waited until I couldn't hear them anymore, tucking it somewhere in the back of my mind that there were three distinct voices, before I slowly pushed the closet door open. They were making their way to the back of the house, and if I could just get to the front door…

My steps were slow as pain racked my body.

Lucifer wanted to come out and play.

I darted out of the room and tucked myself into the corner of the office when I heard a commotion at the front door.

Mario was home.

"Christ, Rick, give me a hand." His key was scraping the lock as he grunted and mumbled to his best friend.

The door finally opened and I heard him laugh as something hard hit the ground. Likely the full weight of his body. I could only assume Rick had helped him back to his feet, because when I peeked out the door, they were headed my way.

"What the—"

I pulled Mario into the office and slapped a hand over his mouth.

"I told you he wouldn't be home yet. We should've handled him at the bar," a voice muttered.

"We never would have made it out alive. Now be quiet. Let's handle the wife and baby."

I lifted three fingers. Hoping that, despite his inebriated state, my husband would understand my meaning. It took a moment, but his eyes finally cleared and a newfound rage took over.

"What do you mean you lost her?"

Metro had somehow lost Mags on their way to me. She was an issue I didn't need right now. The west was breathing down my neck. JP wasn't relenting and it was clear he wouldn't anytime soon. Once I handled all this bullshit, I'd be a better husband. It was time I did what was right.

No more women. No more booze. Just making amends. My son was almost here, and I needed to be the kind of man he could look up to.

In a few short months, Isabella had turned New York into a formidable city. We'd gotten the attention of the *capo dei capi*. He wanted a meeting to see how our family could benefit Italy. He didn't come to the States often, but his interest solidified our place at the top.

"Christ, Rick, give me a hand." The key wouldn't go in the lock. "Another fucking night locked in my prison," I slurred out and regretted my words almost immediately.

Rick moved fast, opening the door and shoving me inside with a laugh. Landing on my ass, I gave him the finger as he closed the door on me. Then I pushed to my feet and wandered aimlessly towards my bedroom.

"What the—" I hissed out as I was pulled into my office with a hand over my mouth.

Isabella was in a silk nightgown, her large belly pushing against me. I was confused one second, murderous another. She appeared unharmed as she lifted three fingers. And I understood instantly. Three men.

They wanted to hurt Isabella and my son… because of me.

I tucked her away under my desk, just as the door started to open. I moved fast, attacking like a madman. I'd disarmed and knocked out two of them before the third even realized what was happening. The last fucker refused to go down as easily. We went blow for blow while the other two started to come to. Blood coated the floor and my knuckles were torn open. It wasn't until Isabella whimpered that I came back to reality.

One of the men had her pinned to his chest. His gun against her temple. I stared at them in horror. "No!"

Isabella held on to her belly, her face twisted, her expression pained.

"Wouldn't I be doing you a favor?" His Italian accent hinted at his identity. "You don't care about this bitch."

I could sense someone walk up behind me. I took a punch to the gut, then the nose, the repeated blows forcing me to my knees. A bunch of fucking cowards hidden by masks except *him.*

"Y-your father. Wants. Peace."

JP—the fucking asshole—smirked. "Didn't you hear? The old bastard's dead. I'm the fucking king now." He glanced at Isabella. "And once they cut that baby out of her, she'll be my whore." He nodded and motioned for one of the men to follow him. They disappeared down the hall as my door closed.

When I get my hands on that motherfucker…

"Mario, th-the baby's coming," Isabella whined, her knees buckling as she dropped closer to the floor.

"You're both fucking dead." My hands twitched, needing to kill the two fuckers threatening my wife. "Isabella, look at me."

She peered up at my face, hers riddled with agony.

I had to make this right.

"Shoot the bitch!" one shouted as she called out for them to wait.

"Mario, I love you. I know you never wanted this, me, but I still love you." She stopped to scream in pain, and the man holding her seemed conflicted. "Mario," she whispered, catching my attention.

And then I saw it. My opening and my wife's quick planning.

I elbowed him in the face and ducked to my right, seconds before Isabella's gun discharged. I didn't hesitate, lunging for the man at her back and slamming my full weight into him. I subdued the fucker easy enough, but Isabella had other plans. She groaned in agony while keeping her grip firm on the gun.

She smiled at him. "Rot in hell, *bastardo.*" His body dropped at the same time that hers folded over.

I moved quickly, helping her to the ground and pulling up her nightgown. "Oh, fuck."

"Whatever you do, make sure my son is okay," Isabella commanded, and only then did I notice the puddle of blood underneath her.

"You're both going to be okay," I assured her, despite knowing how grim the situation was. I refused to let her die the way her mother had. I held my wife's face, staring deeply into her eyes. "I love you, Isabella." And I meant every word of it.

As she gave birth to our son on the floor of my office, so many images of a future without them flashed in my mind. I knew I'd spend the rest of my days making it up to her. I'd love her and my family until I died. Whatever I did in life, it would be for their benefit. For my family. Because this woman owned my heart.

My son was perfect. Something that helped to soothe my mistaken belief that one of my closest confidants had died that day. But in his own words, Mark needed a lot more than some *west coast trash to take him out.*

I'd fallen into a peaceful new routine with my husband, son, and friend at my side. When Mario admitted how he really felt about me, it made a broken part of me feel whole while his promise to be a better man hung heavy in the air.

Only time would tell if there was an ounce of truth in his words.

And I sure as hell wouldn't make it easy on him. Or his whore. Serafina had returned for her wedding. The woman was gorgeous, and I could understand what Mario saw in her. I didn't ask about her child. But when she met Lucifer, she cried and told me everything. It had been a little boy and he was left with a couple who couldn't have children of their own. They'd spoil and comfort him, give him the family she couldn't. She refused to tell Rick, and as I watched the way he acted around her, I understood why. She didn't have to tell me. Whatever transpired between them was bad. Curiosity left me to wonder if Mario knew…

At the same time, I didn't care. She'd made her bed; she could lie in it… with anyone but my husband. Call me ruthless. But for the first time in my entire marriage, I was taking what I wanted. What I deserved.

And Mario catered to my every need.

For example, the beautiful compound he moved us into the moment Lucifer was released from the hospital. Away from the hustle and bustle of the city. Far enough away to achieve that peace I yearned for. But close enough Mario could be *capo*.

My husband was known to be a cruel man. To me, he became more than that. A lover. A friend. A companion. And my son was a spitting image of his father. Lucky had Mario's dark hair and smoldering eyes.

"Earth to Isabella," Serafina huffed.

The white dress I bought fit *Fina* perfectly. It was modest and drew attention to the best parts of her. The wedding was taking place in the ballroom of Mario's hotel. We'd stay here tonight, in the penthouses. They were a second home to us, whenever we needed to be closer to the city, and I could even envision my children living here when they got older. I'd always wanted siblings, so I planned to give my children as many as I was physically able. To raise them to support each other and remain close. They needed to be each other's strength if this family stood a chance of maintaining its power.

"You look beautiful." I offered my former rival a genuine smile.

Serafina and I would never be *best* friends. There were certain things you could never forget. And women remembered everything. The wall between us would always be high, but I'd forever be the sniper at the top. With my target in my sights. The whole *keep your enemies close* mentality.

"Thank you. For… everything," she said, and I waved off the sentiment while scooping Lucky into my arms.

"You'll repay me one day." I pressed my son to my chest and left the woman to her own devices.

Her husband-to-be was under Mario's thumb and our hold on the docks was proving to be lucrative. However, I knew better than to turn a blind eye to a coward like Anthony Moretti. I wanted to know his every move and Serafina would give me that.

"Hello, beautiful." Mario greeted me with a smirk. "You know I hired nannies for a reason."

I scoffed. No one would take care of my son but me. I appreciated the help with getting bottles ready, doing the laundry, and all the little things that would take me away from Lucky. But I enjoyed our one-on-one time. He was growing too quickly already.

"Okay. Okay." Mario pulled me against him with our son nestled between us. "This looks amazing, *mi bella*."

I glanced around the large ballroom that was quickly filling with people. Miranda and her husband were approaching, and I could tell by her face she was just as pleased with the event as I was. She pulled me into a hug as our husbands shook hands.

"No," I said as soon as they began chatting. "No business tonight."

"Yes, ma'am." The senator saluted me before escorting his wife to their seats.

"Don't be mad…" Mario whispered against my ear, and I rolled my eyes at him. "But we're staying for the first dance and then I have plans for you."

My husband was handsome. That was never a question. The man of my dreams *if* our marriage hadn't started out like a nightmare. I knew he was trying. There were many nights I woke to him sitting at the end of the bed. His eyes on me and Lucky and a hand on his gun. He was terrified something would happen to us, and he wanted to be ready in case another threat came through the door.

Tensions with the west were at an all-time high. JP had his hands full with the cartel moving north. Mario wanted to hit him when he was at his weakest. The only reason he hadn't was because of Lucky. Because of me. There'd never be peace with the west. But JP's plot to kill me failed. And his brother died in our city. Some would call it even. Others would say we had a leg up. For now, we left JP with the promise that if he came for us, it would mean the end of his entire bloodline.

Frances came up behind Mario with a devious smile on her face. My glare bounced between them before I submitted to my husband's underhandedness. I laughed as Frances took Lucky and whisked him out of the room with an entourage of guards behind them.

Mario escorted me down the aisle towards the arc where Anthony was waiting for his bride. The two men nodded at each other, but the tension was prevalent, as my husband and I took our seats in the front row.

The murmurs in the room increased when the *capo dei capi* made his presence known. His interest in my newfound political ties bolstered our hold on the city but they also came with warnings. One wrong move and power could quickly shift. Marriages were arranged, alliances made, and children produced as the international crime syndicate continued to grow each day. And we all had our parts to play.

The music cued up as Serafina slowly stepped down the aisle with her father at her side. The woman was white as a ghost and looked like she might pass out at any moment. We made eye contact, and she straightened her spine.

You will do this, my glare told her.

The outspoken girl was suddenly meek and mild as she stood in front of Anthony. I could tell her time with the man hadn't been favorable. Sadly—for her—I didn't give a damn. I owned her now just as much as Mario owned her husband.

"Penny for your thoughts," I muttered as Mario sat tense at my side.

"She looks gorgeous." He sighed and I gritted my teeth. "The picturesque bride."

"It's not too late. You have your son." I flicked my hair over my shoulder. "Make the order. Kill me and Anthony. And get everything you've ever wanted." My teeth threatened to break under the pressure of my jaw.

"She was never the woman for me. I don't think I even wanted her to be. She was the unattainable, a challenge, since I was betrothed to you." Mario grabbed my hand. "I've been the worst husband. I've lied, cheated, and so much worse. The moment I knew you were it for me, I drowned my sorrows in booze and almost got you killed rather than admit my shortcomings."

I had no idea what to say to that. My husband was a man of few words. And those he did say were chosen carefully. I swallowed back my emotion and willed my tears to stay at bay as he kissed each one of my fingertips.

Cheers erupted around us, drawing our attention back to the newly appointed mister and missus.

"Fuck this. I want you to myself," Mario muttered under his breath. Helping me to my feet, he pulled me into the aisle and picked me up bridal-style—the irony wasn't lost on me there.

The entire room of *made men*, associates, and whoever else was in attendance watched as he carried me down the aisle meant for the married couple behind us. But I couldn't see past the determination on my husband's face as he carried me outside and placed me into the car. Mario called out to his men before sliding into the driver's seat. Our security team followed us in their SUVs as we pulled away from the curb.

"I've never taken my wife out on a date. I've committed so many wrongs; it's time I started making them right."

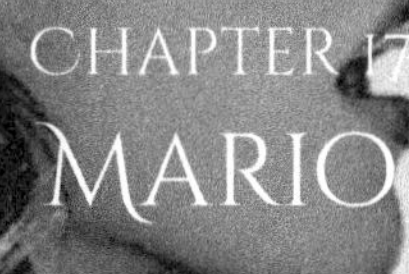

I was a father. I had an heir. My legacy would continue, and with that, I knew I had to do better. I had to *be* better.

Isabella had taken our family to an entirely different realm than I ever thought possible. She maintained an image that propelled us to new heights. All while I lied, cheated, and broke her heart. We'd even gotten the attention of Italy and had basically become untouchable. The *capo dei capi* made it clear… the west needed to stay on their side of the fucking country.

My son was several months old now and he was a good baby. He barely cried, was twice as big as the charts predicted, and the kid adored his mother. I couldn't blame him, though. The woman was a wonder.

His birthday was a few months away, but Isabella was already planning it. She wanted his first year to be a celebration of his life. She also wanted to give back. Our son was spoiled and would grow up with a life of luxury. That said, Isabella wanted him to learn that not everyone was as fortunate. His first birthday was going to be about him as well as those who weren't as blessed. Donations would be made to the local children's hospital in his name.

The moment JP Ragetti entered my home, the moment I saw his men pointing a gun at my wife, it hit me. Isabella was my everything, and the bastard knew it. One glance and he saw my reality come crashing down on me. Things could've ended that day. I've been better for her ever since. I've shown her what I felt all along. And for her, for my family, I'd do whatever I had to do to make sure we fucking *thrived*.

Which meant I had some loose ends to tie up. Mark's thirst for revenge enlivened him. In the months since his recovery, the man grew stronger. Faster. Angrier. With a hair trigger. It left me with two options: I could put him down or I could use him.

Today, I dropped the leash and let him run wild. While I didn't like leaving Lucifer and Isabella alone, especially without Mark to keep an eye on them, this was something we needed to do. JP thought he'd gotten away with threatening me. As if I would allow that to happen.

Instead of backing down, we'd flown across the country, reserved ourselves to staying in the shadows. I'd had men tracking his movements. But someone as irrational and erratic as JP was hard to pinpoint.

Until *her*.

He came home to his new bride every night. The way he doted on her one minute, then left her cold to fuck a whore was disgusting. Maybe because it was a lot like looking in a mirror. But this wasn't about me right now. It was about *him*.

"Ready?"

Mark nodded while practically jumping from the car.

JP liked to roam the seediest motels in his free time. Especially at night. He enjoyed the endless number of women beckoning him into their rooms, accepting his abuse, and taking his money. It was time for him to be caught with his pants down.

I pressed an ear to the door and could hear the sound of running water. The shower. Moving quickly and quietly, we disengaged the lock and stepped inside. The room was empty, except for the stench of cigarette smoke and cheap perfume. Mark positioned himself in one corner, out of direct view, as I lowered myself onto a chair. And we waited… until the water was tapped off and the bathroom door swung open.

"Clean yourself up. Then I want you to crawl out of this room on your fucking knees." JP's voice carried into the room before the man himself appeared with a hooker in tow. "The fuck…?"

"Sit. Now." I nodded at the empty chair opposite me, the barrel of my gun trained on his forehead.

"You're fucking dead," JP snarled as Mark cocked his own gun.

"Listen… or one of us certainly will be."

"Did you really think you could threaten me? My wife… my unborn child, JP?" I tipped my head to one side and pinned him with a glare. "All this bullshit about the west controlling the east? Yeah, it's done. You're fucking done."

"You can't do shit—"

"Can't I?" I lifted a challenging brow before turning my attention to Mark. "Make the call."

A second later, a woman's scream ripped through the speakerphone. JP stormed to his feet, his eyes bulging out of his head while his wife cried out for him on the other end of the line.

An eye for an eye.

"Rick doesn't have a family or children. Spilling your wife's blood would mean nothing to him." I forced JP back into his seat with my gun pressed into his chin. "Would it kill you to know that she's dead because of you? That your unborn child never got the chance to take its first breath?"

The moment the lines on his forehead creased, I knew my suspicions were confirmed. She was several months pregnant with their second child and the bastard didn't even know it. But my men did. They followed her to her doctor's appointment, barged in and grabbed her before anyone could stop them.

A tooth for a tooth.

She was pleading with him over the phone now. "JP, please! Please! I wanted to confirm it was a boy. I wanted to surprise you! Another son!"

"It's okay, baby." His lips tightened into a thin line as he turned his attention to me again. "What do you want, Mario?"

"I want to give Mark here his revenge." I lifted a shoulder in a half shrug, while JP's eyes flicked to the man behind me. "As you know, I took down the men who shot him, but his cousin was also killed during your attack on my home. I want the names of everyone else involved."

"You're fucking crazy."

"Not nearly as crazy as you must have been. Thinking you could come to my city… attack my family, my men. All while knowing I had the evidence to fucking destroy you. Your father is dead but not those loyal to him. One call. That's all I need to make, and you'll be completely wiped out. Your businesses. Men. Family. All of it."

I waited for his mouth to start forming a reply before I hit play, and Serafina's voice filled the room. My incredible wife had the woman's entire confession recorded. Everything I needed to destroy Anthony and JP was on this little tape.

The thing was… if I did make that call, they'd take control of the west and all of Anthony's affairs. The *capo de capi* was a devious and powerful man. He'd want reparations for his involvement. And I couldn't let that happen, but JP didn't need to know that.

"I was so angry at Mario. I didn't care. I knew Anthony would listen. He hates him so much. He called JP, warned him that Sal was coming to New York, warned him of their father's plans to retire early. They did it. JP had men come to meet Anthony. They killed Sal so JP would be the successor."

The Ragettis and the Morettis belonged to me now. JP would do whatever I asked of him, and I'd keep Italy off our heels. We brokered a deal that earned me a percentage from the businesses, and he agreed to never set foot in New York without my permission.

I pushed up from my chair, prepared to put this night behind me, when JP called out my name.

"Mario… Be careful. Rats live in New York too. Right. Under. Your fucking nose."

The fucker was trying to get under my skin, and I didn't have the time or the patience for the rantings of a man who'd clearly been bested.

Truth was I felt sorry for his kids more than anything else. The guy was off his rocker. But it wasn't my problem. I got my money. I locked down peace. I would make sure JP stayed on his goddamn leash and I'd muzzle Anthony Moretti.

One down, one to go. Now that JP and Anthony were handled, I needed to find Mags.

S *everal years later*

"Sienna! Put that down!"

My daughter glared at me, her arms raised with the plastic bat clutched in her hands aimed at her brother's head.

The term *fighting like cats and dogs?* Yeah, not my children. Lucky and Sienna were like two little demons hellbent on destroying each other. Since the day she'd been born, Sienna had been my wild child while Lucky remained my constant shadow— the kid would take over for me tomorrow if he could. Which was difficult for his sister to accept.

Sienna didn't think it was fair that her brother would be handed the keys to the kingdom just because he was the firstborn son. Isabella was working on teaching the girl that women could rule this life. But my little hellion didn't care. She wanted it all for herself.

"Sienna! That dress better not be dirty!" Isabella walked onto the patio, holding Octavia in her arms. "I swear to God…"

Sienna glanced down at her outfit, straightened out a few wrinkles, and went right back to beating on her brother. Our house was a mess. Our children were a mess. And I loved every second of it. These kids kept me on my toes.

"One more?" Isabella looked up at me with hope in her eyes.

Today was Octavia's baptism and *il famiglia* would be coming back to the compound to celebrate after the ceremony. Caterers and staff bustled about while dodging the two kids pummeling each other in the middle of the yard. Our youngest was the opposite of her siblings. She was quiet. Sweet. Reserved.

"One more." I nodded as Frances came up behind my wife to grab the baby.

"Good." Isabella patted her stomach, a knowing smirk lighting up her face.

"Now? You're…?"

She nodded and I pulled her in for a kiss.

"Ew! Gross!" Lucky bellowed at us, his sister echoing the sentiment a second later.

"I can't wait for the day you two fall in love." Isabella smiled, then turned serious. "Inside, right now, young lady!"

Sienna glanced down at her now dirty dress with a grimace. "It's his fault!" she whined before stomping over to her mother.

"What have I told you over and over again?" Isabella grabbed our daughter's hand before dragging her inside.

"A lady always dresses the part," Sienna huffed.

"Exactly. You dress appropriately to beat on your brother—"

The door closed behind them, cutting off the rest of my wife's reprimand.

"She started it." Lucky sighed. "It's not my fault she's a girl and I'm a boy."

"I know. But think about it this way." Staring into eyes that matched my own, I smiled. "If you can get your sister on your side, you'll have one hell of an ally when you take over."

"Is she in a lot of trouble?" he asked, and I raised a questioning brow. "You told me to stay away from Gio Moretti and I did. Sienna caught him trying to get a group of kids to beat me up at school and—"

This was news to me. Anthony and Fina had two children, with a third on the way, and there was no love lost between our broods.

"And?"

"And… his arm might be broken."

Maybe it was because I was *capo* of the New York syndicate. Maybe it was because I was a sick man. But the thought of my daughter standing up for her brother made me smile.

The years continued to pass, and as my children got older, I sometimes wondered how I'd been so lucky. I couldn't stop smiling as my family grew and my wife became an even more powerful force. I loved watching Isabella work a room, even with several sullen teenagers in tow. People were enthralled by her and she was all mine.

"Congratulations on such a beautiful family." Metro glanced around the party. "You're a lucky man."

Sienna was growing into a beautiful woman and we wanted to give her the sort of party to match. She'd long outgrown her childish fancies and was the picture of poise and elegance—mixed with an Italian temper.

"As are you." I shook his hand while my gaze bounced to his wife and son.

"Please. She's a gold-digging whore who raised a spoiled brat," he grunted, eyeing the woman in question as she knocked back another cocktail—three sheets to the wind and the party had barely started. "Jeff! Knock it off!" Metro shouted at his son before turning back to me. "The whining… it never ends. At his age, I was preparing to take my seat in Philly. That kid? He's just a little asshole."

Cringing internally, I patted his back. "Well, I appreciate you making the drive."

"Of course, of course," he hummed and the tilt of his smirk drew my attention. "I come bearing gifts." Metro paused before motioning to the table. "Sienna's is there, but I have something for you as well."

"You found her." It wasn't a question.

"In the gutter." He shook his head. "She's an absolute mess. Drug addict. If the track marks running up and down her arms didn't clue ya in, the missing teeth and scratching sure as fuck would."

"Jesus." I'd cleaned her up and helped her overcome her addiction before she'd turned on me. "I don't care."

"I figured as much." Metro gestured for his right hand to step forward. "Here's the address if you'd like to send Mark ahead of you."

I clamped an arm on his shoulder. "Thank you, my friend."

Sienna glared at her brother, annoyed that he'd even bothered to show up. She stomped her designer heels in his direction before giving him a piece of her mind. We couldn't hear her, but her face said it all. Jeff—Metro's son—was nipping at her heels and she turned that same glare on him, sending the poor kid back a few steps.

We both rolled our eyes. "Teenagers," I scoffed.

"Your daughter is going to give these boys a run for their money." Metro laughed while gesturing to Lucky.

"Don't I know it." I grinned.

I excused myself and went in search of my wife to spend the remainder of the party with my family.

After everyone had returned to their respective homes for the evening, I followed Isabella into the shower. I helped her undress and she smirked as the material slipped from her body. She reached into the stall and started the hot water, then helped me out of my clothes.

"You have places to be," she said more than asked. Isabella didn't miss anything. She knew something was up.

"Yes. And right now, it's buried deep inside you."

She squealed as I picked her up and hauled her into the shower, getting lost in the feel of my beautiful wife.

Mags had evaded me for years now. She could wait a little longer.

My hands firmly gripped her neck, the delicate muscles pulling taut beneath my hold. And I watched on as exhaustion was slowly replaced by terror. A man of my power—caliber—didn't tolerate a woman's disobedience. Their punishment was often simple, but in this case, she deserved the worst.

She'd tried to throw me to the wolves. The mutts constantly sniffing around, wanting to snuff out my reign. Being the head of *il famiglia* guaranteed me enemies. But it shouldn't be those closest to me putting the blade in my back.

"I don't believe your fuckin' lies," I snarled in her face, her eyes begging me to let her go. "You little bitch! How could you do this to me?" I flexed my hand and dumped her body at my feet as she heaved in labored breaths.

"Y-you don't kill women, Mario. I know you!" She curled up on her side, her makeup smeared and her sobs pathetic.

Gripping her hair, I tugged her head back, forcing her to look me in the face. "You *did* fucking know me. Which meant you should've kept your fuckin' mouth shut." I released my grip for a second time—the mere thought of her touch made me sick. "I want to know every-fucking-thing you told him."

"N-nothing. I swear, Mario!" Her lies flowed so easily I wanted to snap her neck.

I picked up a chair and threw it across the room.

"All right, calm down." Rick stood to the side—my best friend sounded amused where I was heated. "Either do it or don't, but let's go."

Why was it that those closest to me had the sharpest knives? All the women in my life had let me down. *She* was no different. The moment I looked away, she tried running to another city. To another boss.

But my reach far surpassed New York, and Philly was a friend. Thankfully.

Rick wasn't much better. He'd never settled down but had his own crew and his own businesses he was running. Something seemed to change in him. He left for Italy and when he came back, he moved to Jersey. His reasoning? To allow me the space I needed to run my crew and manage my family. He claimed he wanted his own piece of the pie. For himself. So I let him.

As my right hand, the power I'd amassed transferred to him. It was my gift, in exchange for his years of loyal service. He had no heirs, so my kids would be the future. He'd made his own way and was successful, but the friend I knew was gone. He would attend various familial events, stepping up when needed, especially for business that involved Jersey. Outside of that, the man had become a stranger.

Rick. Serafina. Anthony. The west. None of them mattered. I had my family, and my wife had ensured we had control over everything and everyone.

"I just wanted your attention, Mario. That's all." She started kissing my shoes. "You're my everything. W-when you sent me away, I just wanted your attention."

"Well, you fuckin' got it, didn't you?"

"I'm sorry! She doesn't make you happy and that's why you

spent all your time with me! I acted out and I wanted to apologize! But you wouldn't let me."

"Those drugs must be eating away at your brain. Acting like you're *someone* to me."

She wept harder when my hands combed through her hair, gripping tight before I dragged her into the back room as she fought against me.

"You fucked up."

"Please, I need to tell you… just let me explain!"

I deposited her crying, lying ass into the center of the locked room and smiled when she glanced at the drain dug into the cement floor. Then I lifted my hand, realization settling over her face as she stared down the barrel of my gun.

"Please… if you kill me… you'll never find her. Your daughter."

I froze to the spot. "The fuck did you just say?"

"Y-you heard me. I fled because you wouldn't listen. I tried to tell you and you dismissed me." She hung her head in shame. "So I tried to get payback. Instead, I gave birth alone. Your daughter almost died."

"You're fucking lying."

"Where is she?" The sound of my wife's voice had me glancing over one shoulder. "Tell me, Mags. Where is she?" Isabella urged.

The way Mags's lips curled into a snarl had my finger teetering dangerously close to the trigger. But her words gave me pause— whether they were truth or just another lie had yet to be determined.

"Where, Mags?" My wife stood strong at my side.

A child born out of wedlock. Yet the look in my wife's eyes told me that she didn't care. She'd take the girl in and raise her as her own.

"Nowhere you'll fucking find her." Mags spat at Isabella's feet. "She's mine. A little piece of your husband that belongs to me."

Isabella burst out laughing. "Interesting. Well, let me make you a promise. I'll find her. And I will ensure she's loved. That she has a chance at knowing happiness. A chance to be a reputable young woman, unlike her mother." Then my wife turned towards one of my men standing at the back of the room. "Find her daughter. Do whatever you need to do. Just get it done as soon as possible."

I nodded once, ignoring Mag's cries as I pulled Isabella out the door with me. The woman never ceased to amaze me. I had no doubt that Mark had given her a heads up once he'd returned to the compound.

I paused in the street to light a cigarette. And enjoyed the feel of the nicotine filling my lungs. That was another declaration made by my wife. No smoking in the house. And I knew better than to argue with her over a minor inconvenience.

"Let's go. I want to go home." Isabella slid into the car and I quickly climbed in after her. "I meant what I said in there. That girl belongs with us. God knows what she went through already. If we don't find her, I can't even begin to imagine what will become of her…"

She didn't have to say it. We both knew the implication. If Mags was living in a gutter, so was my daughter…

Four children later, I was content with my life. I continued to give back to those less fortunate while focusing on my family. The kids grew so damn fast, and before I knew it, they were preparing to start lives of their own.

Sienna was the most like me. She loved with everything she had. Her infatuation with our *adopted* son was toxic and concerning, but I knew my girl would overcome it. Sienna wasn't capable of breaking. And if she did—family or not—I'd make Apollo sorry for every part he had in it. Then I'd happily watch as she rebuilt herself.

Lucky was like his father—the man my husband became later in life. His hard work and dedication to our family and his fiancée, Mirabella, proved that.

Over time, Serafina and I had become real friends because I felt sorry for her. She was suffering enough for her past transgressions. After a couple of years, she decided she wanted to meet her son. Who seemingly disappeared after his adopted family was killed in a car crash. Considering how much she lost and how cruel her husband was, I truly pitied her. Then, when Anthony sent Mirabella to Italy for an extended visit, a part of Fina broke. She became a shell of who she was.

First a son, then a daughter.

Marco, my youngest, was Mario in his early years. My son was a whore, and I was slowly losing my patience with the boy. I had a feeling a woman was going to knock him on his ass and I couldn't wait to be there to see it.

My Octavia was something else entirely. We protected her because of her perceived innocence… However, something about that part of her felt wrong. There were several instances where I watched a different person step into the light. One day, the real woman would break free, and when her true colors showed, I was certain we'd all be terrified.

I reminded my husband every day of who he used to be. What he'd done. *Because, ladies, there was nothing wrong with reminding them of their place.* And every day he made it up to me.

"We have a problem." Mark stepped into my gardens.

"Dead end?" I asked, digging through the soil with my hands.

He'd spent the last few years following the trail of used needles and bad decisions Mags left in her wake. The only reason the woman was breathing was because we were hoping she would eventually slip up and lead us back to the girl. Instead, Mags dropped into one gutter after another. Never giving us anything other than more lies. Like she was enjoying watching Mario suffer.

"Overdose. And I got nothing." Mark shook his head, knowing all of our leads were now dry.

My heart broke for that little girl that was probably unloved. Had Mags done the right thing and given her up? Or had she dragged that child through the hell she'd created for herself? Mario had spent the last several years with a silent pain he didn't share with me.

Each year. Each lead. He was losing hope.

Something inside me said the girl wasn't dead. Mags was cruel and an absolute mess, but I could feel it. That child was growing into a woman, and one day we'd find her. One day we'd make up for lost time and the wrongs she more than likely suffered. I just hoped that when she did come into our lives, she didn't bring another storm with her.

My family was my everything, and I'd do whatever it took to ensure they succeeded. Even if I had to prove to Mags's daughter that tough love was the best medicine to make up for lost time. I prayed she was found and that we could save her.

However, none of us were prepared for the torrential downpour that same little girl would bring into our lives. Just like all the other storms, we'd get through it. Together.

The End.

About the Author

Corporate sales by day, closet romance novelist at night—Dahlia Reign has always had an unparalleled taste for dreamy alpha-men. In her youth, Dahlia had journals by the stacks that she used to jot down her innermost thoughts; subsequently, turning them into romantic stories. Now, years later and with her picturesque alpha-man at her side, she's taken the literary world by storm. Her man, her pittie and an overactive imagination mixed with her bleeding heart—she's set off to tell the world her stories. Buck up and grab a bandaid, shit's about to get heavy.

www.TheDahliaReign.com

ALSO BY DAHLIA REIGN

<u>Agostino Crime Family Series</u>

Original Sin: A Prequel

Contracted to the Devil: Book One

Clever as the Devil: Book Two

Beautiful Deception: Book Three

And Twice as Twisted: Book Four

Bittersweet Revenge: Book Five

<u>La Reina de Escorpiones Duet</u>

Infinite Sorrow: Book One

Endless Deceit: Book Two

<u>Standalones</u>

The Sins of Our Father

www.TheDahliaReign.com